# The Princess Diaries

## Yearbook 2007

First published 2006 by Macmillan Children's Books
a division of Macmillan Publishers Limited
20 New Wharf Road, London N1 9RR
Basingstoke and Oxford
www.panmacmillan.co.uk

Associated companies throughout the world

ISBN-13: 978-1-4050-8885-5
ISBN-10: 1-4050-8885-0

Text copyright © Meg Cabot 2006
Illustrations copyright © Nicola Slater 2006

The right of Meg Cabot and Nicola Slater to be
identified as the author and illustrator of this work
has been asserted by them in accordance with
the Copyright, Designs and Patents Act 1988.

1 3 5 7 9 8 6 4 2

A CIP catalogue record for this book is available from
the British Library.

Design by John Fordham
Printed and bound in Belgium by Proost

# The Princess Diaries

### Yearbook 2007

# MEG CABOT

MACMILLAN

# CONTENTS

# Dear Princess,

Ever since I found out I am the heir to a small European principality (Genovia, population 50,000), and had my diaries published and two movies made out of the story of my life, everyone wants me to talk about the whole princess thing. As you probably know, I am kind of a reluctant princess – and would actually much rather be a normal girl – BUT I do take my majestic duties very seriously. So may I introduce you to THE PRINCESS DIARIES YEARBOOK, which should keep you very busy – and royally entertained – in 2007!

Enjoy!

## Love, Mia

Amelia Mignonette Grimaldi Thermopolis Renaldo,
Princess of Genovia

# Princess Mia
## TELLS IT LIKE IT IS

Check out some of Mia's wisest sayings.
They'll help you develop the Princess Attitude –
which is actually the most important part of
being a true princess.

> Princesses always put their best face forward. So you've got a huge zit, a D-minus in Algebra, and the guy you secretly adore was spotted at a party last night with some other girl. Never let them see any of it bothering you! But don't be fake. Concentrate on what's good in your life, not on the bad stuff.

> When they lose, princesses don't let anyone know it bothers them. Instead, they go home and pour out all their hateful, jealous feelings into their diary. Princesses don't want any pity.

True princesses are never purposefully rude or mean to others (even cheerleaders!) And random acts of kindness – offering to go to the movies with the new girl whom no one likes, letting your best friend borrow your tiara to wear on her cable-access television show – are all extremely princessy.

Just because you are kind does not mean you have to be a pushover. Don't let other people tell you what to do – unless what they are proposing is for your own good, like taking Algebra – particularly when you feel what they are proposing is morally or legally wrong. Remember, it's princesslike to be assertive; it is unprincesslike purposefully to hurt yourself or others.

Say 'Good Morning' to the girls you hate the most. When they mock you, smile sweetly – but pityingly – at them. Do this enough times and they will become confused and wary of you. It really works, princess!

# ACT LIKE A PRINCESS

Since Mia found out she was heir to the throne of Genovia, she has been attending long and gruelling princess lessons with Grandmere: renowned expert on all things princess. Now it's your turn to be Grandmere's pupil . . .

## Introduction to Etiquette
### by Clarisse Renaldo, Dowager Princess of Genovia

### PRINCESS POSTURE

*Stand Like a Princess*

If you wish to be treated like a princess, it is important that you look like one. Princesses never slouch. A princess stands tall at all times. Picture a string coming out from the top of your head. Imagine someone is pulling that string, keeping your neck erect, your chin up!

*Walk Like a Princess*

A princess does not shuffle, skip or saunter. She strides confidently, with her head held high (remember the string!), her gaze straight ahead and her arms relaxed by her sides (except, of course, when she is holding a purse or small *chien*).

### INTRODUCTIONS TO ROYALS

When meeting royalty for the first time, commoners must bow or curtsy as they are introduced.

*The perfect curtsy*

Place your left foot behind your right, and bend slightly at the knees, then stand up straight again. See? So simple.

### INTRODUCTIONS TO NON-ROYALS

When you are introduced to someone for the first time, you should smile, look the person in the eye, and extend your right hand. Say, 'Hello, I am Clarisse Renaldo, Dowager Princess of Genovia' (or whatever your name happens to be). When shaking hands, exert a confident, not overpowering, grip. You are a princess, not a wrestler.

## EAT LIKE A PRINCESS

*Formal dining dos*

- Always wait until everyone is present at the table before taking your seat.
- Always place your napkin upon your lap.
- Always wait until your hostess has lifted her fork before beginning to eat.
- Remove seeds, bones, or stones from your mouth using your fingers (discreetly), and lay them on the side of your plate (not under the table).
- Use your fingers to eat foods such as potato chips, sandwiches and corn on the cob. Be sure to wipe your fingers on a napkin after each bite – DO NOT LICK THEM.
- When you are finished, lay your knife and fork across your plate, then wait for your hostess to rise before leaving the table.

*Formal dining don'ts*

- Do not speak when your mouth is full.
- Do not cut all your meat (or any food) into bite-sized portions before you begin eating. Cut off only what you intend to put in your mouth at that time.
- Do not suck up the ends of spaghetti. It should be twirled in small portions on the end of the fork, against your spoon or the edge of the plate.
- Do not take huge mouthfuls of anything, no matter how good.

## PRINCESS IN WRITING

Thank-you notes never go out of style, and are never unwelcome. If someone gives you a gift, it is most impolite not to send a thank-you note – and remember: *manners matter!*

The note should be handwritten, preferably on monogrammed royal stationery. It should sound personal and sincere and mention the gift in the body of the note, otherwise the giver might think you just photocopied the note and sent the same one to everyone.

# SWEET SIXTEEN

*Princess Mia doesn't always have the best of luck with parties, so even though it's her sweet sixteenth, she doesn't want a birthday bash. As usual, Grandmere has other ideas, and thinks a reality TV special is just the thing in order to celebrate royally.*
*Will Mia be able to stop Grandmere's plan? Will her friends ever forgive her if she does stop it, since it involves them all taking the royal jet to Genovia for an extravaganza the like of which would turn Paris Hilton green with envy? Why can't Mia get what she really wants: an evening alone with Michael?*
*Find out more in this hilarious*
*THE PRINCESS DIARIES story . . .*

## Wednesday, April 28, 9 p.m., Albert Einstein High School Gymnasium

'So Lana's dad rented the Sultan of Brunei's ten-million-dollar yacht for the night and had Lana and her friends driven out into international waters so they could drink without getting in trouble.'

This is what Lilly just called to tell me.

'Lilly,' I whispered. 'You know you aren't supposed to call me on my cellphone. It is for emergency use only.'

'You don't think this is an emergency, Mia? Lana's dad renting the Sultan of Brunei's yacht like that? That is a throwdown. He is basically telling your grandmother to bring it.'

'I don't have the slightest idea what you're talking about.' Because I don't. 'And I have to go. I'm at a PTA meeting, for crying out loud.'

'Oh God.' I can hear the soundtrack for Altar Boyz in the background. Ever since Lilly started going out with J.P. Reynolds-Abernathy the Fourth, she has got way into soundtracks from musicals, because J.P.'s dad is a theatre producer and J.P. can get free tickets to any Broadway show he wants, and all of the off-Broadway ones too. And even the off-off-Broadway ones. 'I forgot you had to go to that stupid thing. Sorry I'm not there with you. But . . . well, you know.'

I did know. Lilly was serving the last week of a grounding her parents instituted after she was brought home by the NYPD for attacking Andy Milonakis – this kid from downtown whose cable-access television show was picked up by MTV – with a Dojo's side salad. Lilly believes Andy getting a basic cable deal instead of her is a travesty of justice, because her own local show, *Lilly Tells It Like It Is*, is so much better (in her opinion), as it isn't simply entertaining, but also highlights facts she feels her viewers ought to be aware of. Such as the fact that the US's decision to withhold $34 million from the United Nations Population Fund will lead to two million unwanted pregnancies, 800,000 induced abortions, 4,700 maternal deaths and 77,000 infant and child deaths worldwide.

Whereas a typical episode of Andy's show features him holding a jar of peanut butter in one hand, a jar of salsa in the other, then making the jars dance with each other.

Lilly is also peeved that Andy is deceiving the American public by allowing them to think he is just a kid, when we both saw him coming out of dba, which is a bar in the East Village that cards. So how did he get in there if he isn't at least twenty-one?

This is what she asked him when she saw him eating a falafel at Dojo's Health Restaurant on St Mark's Place, and why she claims she was forced to hurl her side salad at him, drenching him in tahini dressing and causing him to call the cops on her.

Thankfully the Drs Moscovitz talked Andy's legal team out of pressing charges, explaining that Lilly has been experiencing some anger issues since their recent separation.

But that didn't stop them from grounding her.

'So how's the meeting going?' Lilly asked. 'Have they got to the you-know-what part yet?'

'I wouldn't know, because I'm too distracted, talking to YOU,' I whispered. I had to whisper, because I was sitting in a folding chair in the middle of a row of very uptight-looking parents. Being New Yorkers, they were all, of course, very

15

well dressed, with Prada accessories. But being New Yorkers, they were also all angry about the fact that someone was using a cellphone while someone else – namely Principal Gupta – was up at the podium, speaking. Also, of course, that Principal Gupta was basically saying she couldn't guarantee that their kids would get into Yale or Harvard, which was making them madder than anything. At $20,000 a year – which is how much tuition at AEHS costs – New York parents expect some return for their investment.

'Well, I'll let you go now, so you can get back to work,' Lilly said. 'But just FYI: Lana's dad had her flown to the yacht on the sultan's helicopter, so she could make a spectacular entrance.'

'I hope one of the blades cut her head off as she was getting out of it because she forgot to duck,' I whispered, avoiding the glare of the lady in front of me, who had turned in her seat to give me a dirty look for talking while Principal Gupta was giving everyone some very important information about the percentage of AEHS graduates who get into Ivy League colleges.

'Well,' Lilly said, 'no, that didn't happen. But I heard her Azzedine Alaia skirt flew up over her head and everyone saw that she was wearing a thong.'

'Goodbye, Lilly,' I said.

'I'm just telling you. Turning sixteen is a big deal. You only do it once. Don't blow it by having one of your stupid loft parties with Cheetos, and Mr G as a DJ.'

'Goodbye, Lilly.'

I hung up just as the lady in the seat in front of me turned around to hiss, 'Would you please put away that . . .'

But she never got to finish, because Lars, who was sitting next to me, casually opened his suit jacket, revealing his sidearm. He was only reaching for a Listerine PocketPak, but the sight of his Glock 9 caused the lady's eyes to widen. She closed her mouth and turned back around in her seat very quickly.

Having an armed bodyguard follow you around everywhere you go can be a total pain in the butt, particularly when it comes to finding private time with your boyfriend.

But there are moments, like that one, when it can actually rock.

Then Principal Gupta asked if there was any outstanding business, and I threw my arm into the air.

Principal Gupta saw me raise my hand. I know she did.

But she totally ignored me, and called on some freshman's mother who wanted to know why the school wasn't doing more to prepare students for the SATs.

She went on to ignore me until she'd answered everyone else's questions. I can't really say that this shows the kind of commitment to youth-oriented issues I'd like to see in my educators, but who am I to complain? Just the president of the student council, is all.

Which is why, after Principal Gupta finally called on me, I saw a lot of parents gathering their Gucci briefcases and Zabar's shopping bags and getting ready to leave. Because who wants to listen to the president of the student council?

'Um, hi,' I said, uncomfortably aware of the number of gazes – even if they were only half listening – on me. I may be a princess and all, but I'm still not used to the whole public-speaking thing, despite Grandmere's best efforts. 'I've been asked by a number of AEHS students to address the Parent–Teacher Association on the issue of our current physical-education curriculum, specifically its emphasis on competitive sports. We feel that spending six weeks learning the finer points of volleyball is a waste of our time and our parents' money. We would prefer our physical-education funds be spent on physical education that is just that: education about our physical well-being. We'd like the gymnasium to be converted to an actual fitness centre, with weight-training equipment and stationary bikes for spin classes, as well as space for Pilates and t'ai chi. And for our physical-education instructor to act as both a personal trainer and health specialist, who will work with each student individually to create a personal workout and health programme targeted to their specific health needs, whether they be weight loss, increase in muscle tone, stress reduction or simply improved overall health. As you can see –' I pulled out a pile of paper I'd been keeping in my backpack and began passing the sheets around – 'we've assessed the overall costs involved in implementing this kind of health programme and found that it is much more cost efficient than our current physical-education curriculum, if you take into account the staggering amount of money you'll be paying to your child's physicians for treatment of juvenile-onset diabetes, asthma, high blood pressure and the many other dangerous health conditions caused by obesity.'

SWEET SIXTEEN *continues on page 26*

# PRINCESS BEAUTY

## A Note from Princess Mia

Real princesses always try to look their best — but my best is probably totally different from yours. There are lots of different kinds of beauty. Like those models on magazine covers? A lot of people might hold them up as like the epitome of perfection, but just remember, in France it's considered beautiful not to shave under your arms.

So you see, beauty is really relative.

Princesses, like people, come in all different shapes and sizes. There is no one look that is right for everyone. Having a healthy body is way more important than having a body that looks good in low-rise jeans. And, of course, being a nice person is the most important thing of all.

There's one thing that looks good on everyone, though: confidence. Have confidence in yourself and your look, and others will see the outer beauty as well the inner.

That's what everyone keeps telling me anyway.

## PRETTY PRINCESS

The key to truly regal beauty is simplicity; it is never, ever a good thing to trowel on the make-up to the point where your actual skin colour is no longer visible. Remember, princess, we are NOT trying to look plastic. Boys really do not like the overly made-up look – it confuses and scares them. Less is definitely more. A princess should aim to look healthy and well groomed. To help you achieve this, here are some top tips:

- Always apply make-up in lots of **natural light**. You don't want to over-compensate for poor lighting and end up looking like the bride of Dracula.

- **Never** emphasize your eyes *and* your lips. Go for one or the other. Like, wear smoky eye make-up with a slick of lip balm or transparent gloss. If you're going for dramatic colour on your lips, keep the eyes subtle: nude eye shadow and mascara is all you need.

- Mix a pea-sized amount of foundation with your moisturizer to create a light, easy to wear tinted **moisturizer**, that allows a princess's skin to *breathe*.

- Use a cream or powder highlighter/illuminator/shimmer to create a fresh-faced glow. Dab a tiny amount on the top of your cheekbones and your brow bone (underneath the eyebrow) to highlight your face. You will **sparkle**.

- Do the same on your collarbone and shoulders if they're exposed.

- Mix a bit of the highlighter with your lip balm to create an **iridescent** lip gloss.

- Use a white or pale gold eyeshadow on the inner corner of your eye, or line the inner bottom rim of your eye with a white eye pencil to make you look **wide awake**.

- **Dab** your mascara wand on a bit of tissue before applying to remove any clumps.

- For a dramatic going-out look, wear **false eyelashes**. Princess Mia tells you how on page 21.

- To create **smoky eyes**, line your lash line top and bottom with a small amount of dark brown/grey powder eyeshadow. Extend just beyond your eye, sweeping upwards very slightly at the outer edge of your eye. Then smudge in using a cotton bud. Apply two coats of black mascara to finish.

- Apply a little bit of Vaseline or clear mascara to your lashes for an **everyday** look.

- **Smile** so you can see the apples of your cheeks – this is where you want to apply your blusher, blending outwards. Try apricot and peachy shades for subtle princess prettiness.

- Get rid of any **shininess** in your T-zone with blotting tissues or oil-absorbent paper. Much better than applying layer after layer of powder.

- **Never** outline your lips with a lip liner and then fill in with a contrasting shade of lipstick.

- If you have a **pimple**, dab a tiny bit of concealer on the top of it, rather than on the sides, as this will only serve to emphasize it.

- If you feel that your make-up is looking **cakey**, dab (don't rub) your face very gently with a damp face cloth or with your (clean) fingers.

- When **removing** eye make-up, wipe inwards towards your nose so you don't stretch the delicate skin around your eye.

- It really isn't necessary to wear make-up **everyday**. If you wear it all the time, you'll have nothing saved to wow people with at the weekend!

19

# PAOLO'S PRINCESS ESSENTIALS

What every princess should have in her handbag (besides money, breath mints, emergency tiara and hairbrush):

- Lipstick or gloss
- Pressed powder compact (to get rid of shiny nose)
- Concealer (for dark circles under the eyes due to that light-night romantic tryst, no? Also for blemishes)
- Eye pencil

## Paulo's Top Tip

Keep one of those mini perfume testers in your make-up bag in case of any last-minute dinner engagements. You'll always have it handy and then people will comment: 'Aahh, that Principessa, she always smells like a little flower!'

What every princess should have in her bathroom back home (besides a phone and small television so she can keep abreast of world events even while bathing the royal body):

- Facial cleanser/exfoliator (or use a washcloth, but gently!) and moisturizer
- Astringent/toner/acne medication/beauty masks
- Foundation/tinted moisturizer
- Eyeshadow (no kohl, Paolo spits on kohl!)
- Blusher (natural colour, unless you want to look like a clown)
- Mascara
- Manicure set (nail polish, nail file, nail cutter)
- Hair products (shampoo, conditioner, serum, etc.)
- Shower gel
- Bubble bath

# PAOLO'S
## FIVE-MINUTE MAKEOVER

### From daytime casual to full-on, party glamour

For the princess on-the-go who needs a quick and easy transformation:

1. **Retouch** any areas that need a bit of concealer (your under-eyes, the sides of your nose, any pimples or blotchy bits). Use your fourth (ring) finger to achieve a really light, gentle touch. **Blend well.**

2. Banish any **shine** with a layer of powder.

3. Re-apply **blusher** for an instant healthy glow. (And please, for Paulo, make sure that this is a glow and not a stripe.)

4. Apply **either** your evening eye make-up or lip colour, only one or the other. Remember, a mask works only at Halloween! If using lipstick, apply the first coat, blot with a tissue, then apply second layer. Whatever you're using (lipstick or gloss), make sure you follow your natural lip-line.

5. Apply **highlighter/shimmer** to the top of your cheekbones, the arch of your eyebrows and your collarbone and shoulders. If you have a glittery white/gold eyeshadow, you could use a little of this as an alternative.

**And there you have it!** *Bella!* **And so easy!**

It may take a little practice, but before long you'll have it down, and be ready to waltz the night away within five minutes!

## Princess Mia's Top Tip:

**To apply false eyelashes, first:**

Make up your eyes in your normal fashion (shadow, liner, mascara). You will have a hard time applying these AFTER the lashes are glued on. Next, TRIM the lashes to fit the width of your eyes. False eyelashes are NOT one size fits all. Then apply a SMALL amount of the glue that came with the lashes (remember, you are putting glue NEAR YOUR EYE. USE ONLY SPECIALLY DESIGNED FALSE EYELASH GLUE FOR THIS) and, with tweezers or clean fingers, apply the lashes to your upper lid, making sure to tap them down so that they rest against your real eyelashes.

Don't expect to execute the above move in one try. It will take LOTS of practice before you get it right.

Once you've got it right, and after the glue has dried, gently CURL your lashes with your eyelash curler so the fake ones blend better with your real lashes, then apply another layer of mascara. Blink a few times to make sure the fake lashes stay in place.

**You're good to go!**

21

# PRECIOUS PRINCESS

Many people believe that
gemstones are very powerful.
Make sure you use this guide next time you're
choosing a new gemstone for your tiara!

### Amethyst
Enhances your creativity
and gives you inspiration.

### Aquamarine
Brings out your sensitivity
and makes you more intuitive.

### Diamond
Gives you a clear mind
and happy thoughts.

### Emerald
Makes you lucky in love.

### Garnet
Repels negativity and
guards against sadness.

### Jade
Brings love and
money into your life.

### Moonstone
Gives you peace of mind
and good dreams.

### Opal
The most powerful
healing stone.

### Peridot
Attracts wealth
and success.

### Ruby
Brings contentment and
is also a symbol of love.

### Sapphire
Makes you more perceptive
and is also healing.

### Topaz
Brings happiness and hope.

### Turquoise
Protects and is also the
symbol of friendship.

Over thousands of years
a tradition has developed
associating certain gemstones
with months of the year.
So perhaps you'd rather choose your birthstone
to adorn your crown jewels.

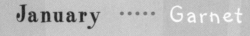

| January | ..... | Garnet |
| February | ..... | Amethyst |
| March | ..... | Aquamarine |
| April | ..... | Diamond |
| May | ..... | Emerald |
| June | ..... | Moonstone |
| July | ..... | Ruby |
| August | ..... | Peridot |
| September | ..... | Sapphire |
| October | ..... | Opal |
| November | ..... | Topaz |
| December | ..... | Turquoise |

# PUZZLED PRINCESS

Can you answer the princess-related questions and fill in the grid?

## ACROSS

1. Fishy Disney princess (5)
5. Pop princess or trailer trash? (7)
6. Princess with a pet raccoon (10)
10. Anne, star of Mia's movies (8)
13. Mia's best friend (5)
14. Ouch! What's under the mattress? (3)

## DOWN

2. TETEUQETI (anagram, 9)
3. Mia's school (initials, 3)
4. Louie is a fat one! (3)
5. Lars is Mia's (9)
6. Mia will save it! (6)
7. William is a real Prince _____ (8)
8. The Princess Diaries 6 (11)
9. Grand princess party (4)
11. Princess house (6)
12. Mia's birthday month (3)

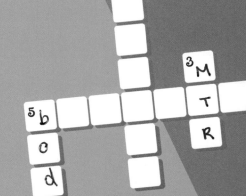

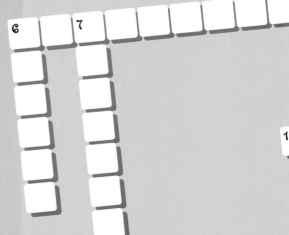

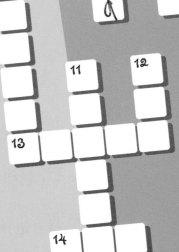

24

For solution see page 92

# PRINCESS WORDSEARCH

Can you find the sixteen hidden princesses?
Words are hidden horizontally, vertically and diagonally -
and run backwards and forwards!

| | | | | | | | | | | | | | | | | | | | | |
|---|---|---|---|---|---|---|---|---|---|---|---|---|---|---|---|---|---|---|---|---|
| A | Y | E | D | A | C | W | E | U | C | E | R | L | A | Y | B | I | M | B | H |
| K | I | C | W | Z | L | C | U | Q | F | D | M | X | P | P | T | P | O | H | X |
| U | X | S | S | R | A | S | X | T | E | N | I | M | S | A | J | U | T | Y | U |
| M | P | T | A | R | R | A | M | X | A | U | R | D | C | Y | D | M | A | E | S |
| K | V | J | G | T | I | W | Y | Z | N | G | Q | B | D | I | A | N | A | E | V |
| Y | X | G | P | Q | S | X | B | A | K | A | B | A | C | P | N | O | T | A | B |
| Y | M | R | Q | I | S | A | W | D | M | S | S | C | L | Z | Q | X | H | T | Z |
| A | L | L | E | R | E | D | N | I | C | O | A | C | J | E | T | M | J | I | Z |
| V | J | K | Q | K | M | V | A | A | F | R | J | U | T | G | T | X | E | D | W |
| V | L | C | H | C | J | O | R | Q | E | C | U | Y | M | S | Q | A | K | B | J |
| T | B | H | F | T | W | T | X | N | U | Z | Z | C | P | F | L | T | X | I | U |
| W | Y | Z | N | U | A | L | C | T | Q | E | H | I | W | D | E | P | W | X | M |
| U | D | Z | C | P | O | R | F | P | K | I | Y | S | J | V | I | T | Q | W | U |
| R | V | T | O | A | V | N | G | N | N | Q | T | B | I | I | A | R | L | Y | E |
| Z | E | E | C | D | R | J | N | Z | C | R | B | T | R | U | W | N | D | F | H |
| E | L | T | T | O | L | O | B | K | O | K | A | B | A | X | Y | B | T | R | E |
| C | I | R | D | G | E | S | L | O | I | H | B | S | S | Y | X | W | H | H | Z |
| S | L | E | E | P | I | N | G | I | A | M | P | F | L | X | N | J | Q | L | U |
| F | H | B | F | Z | R | C | U | V | N | G | L | O | M | V | G | Q | B | R | C |
| H | T | Y | R | N | A | I | Q | L | C | E | G | D | K | A | J | I | I | Z | L |

| ALETA | BOUDICCA | CLEOPATRA | LEIA |
|---|---|---|---|
| ANASTASIA | CAROLINE | DIANA | MIA |
| ARIEL | CINDERELLA | GRACE | ROSAGUNDE |
| BEAUTY | CLARISSE | JASMINE | SLEEPING |

25

For solution see page 92

This information was not met with the kind of enthusiastic response we – meaning my fellow student-council members, Lilly, Tina, Ling Su, and I – had been hoping for. Parents, I noted, tended to look heavenward, and Principal Gupta glanced at her watch.

'Thank you for this, Mia,' she said, holding up the copy of the breakdown I'd given her. 'But I'm afraid what you're proposing would be far too cost prohibitive for us at this time—'

'But as you can see by our projections,' I said desperately, 'if you were to just take a small amount of money away from, say, the Intramural Athletics Fund—'

At this, suddenly everyone was paying attention.

'Not the lacrosse team!' one father in a Burberry raincoat bellowed.

'Not soccer,' cried another, looking up from his BlackBerry with a panicked expression on his face.

'Not cheerleading!' Mr Taylor, Shameeka's dad, gave me a dirty look that would have rivalled one of Grandmere's.

'You see the problem, Mia?' Principal Gupta shook her head.

'But if each team just gave up a little—'

'I'm sorry, Mia,' Principal Gupta said. 'I'm sure you worked very hard on this. But your track record where financial matters are concerned hasn't exactly been the most stellar –' I couldn't believe she'd be so heartless as to bring up the slight miscalculation that had caused me to bankrupt the student government several weeks earlier. Especially considering the fact that, with the help of my grandmother and her tireless work on behalf of the Genovian olive growers, I had more than replenished the empty coffers – 'and I haven't heard any other complaints about our current PE curriculum. I move that we conclude this meeting—'

'I second the motion,' cried Mrs Hill, my Gifted and Talented teacher, in an obvious ploy to get home in time for *Dancing with the Stars*.

'This meeting of the Albert Einstein High School Parent–Teacher Association is adjourned,' Principal Gupta said.

Then she and everybody else booked out of there like winged monkeys were on their tails.

I looked down at Lars, the only person left in the room besides me.

'"The first resistance to social change is to say it's not necessary,"' he said, obviously quoting somebody.

'Sun Tzu?' I asked, since *The Art of War* is Lars's favourite book.

'Gloria Steinem,' he confessed. 'I was reading one of your mother's magazines in the bathroom the other day.' Lars has apparently never heard of the phrase Too Much Information. 'Let's go home, Princess.'

And so we did.

## Wednesday, April 28, 10 p.m., Limo Ride Home

How am I ever going to rule an entire country some day when I can't even get my high school to install a row of stationary bikes in the gym?

## Wednesday, April 28, 10:30 p.m., the Loft

At least I have the comforting words of my boyfriend to soothe my frazzled nerves when I get home after a long day of fighting for the rights of the unathletically inclined students of Albert Einstein High. Even if I hardly ever get to talk to him – except via Instant Messaging – because he's so busy with his college courses, and I'm so busy with Geometry, princess lessons, student council and keeping my baby brother from sticking his tongue in a light socket.

```
SkinnerBx: Do you realize it's only three days
till the big day?
>
FtLouie: What day would that be?
>
SkinnerBx: Your sweet sixteen!
>
```

```
FtLouie: Oh, right. I forgot. Sorry. Stupid school stuff is
bumming me out.
>
SkinnerBx: Poor baby. So what do you want for your
birthday?
>
FtLouie: Just you.
>
SkinnerBx: Are you serious???? Because that can totally be
arranged. Doo Pak is going to be gone for the weekend on a
Korean Student Association campout in the Catskills . . .
```

Yikes! All I meant was that I wanted a little time alone with him – something that seems to happen more and more rarely now that he's opted for accelerated graduation, doing all his coursework in three years instead of four, and now that his parents have split up and all, so that he has to have dinner every Friday night with either his mom or dad so that each of them feels like they're getting their fair share of Michael time.

And, being the supportive girlfriend that I am, I totally understand about Michael's being there for his parents during this stressful time in their lives. Mr Dr Moscovitz doesn't seem to really like his new rental apartment on the Upper West Side very much, even though he lives just a *New York Times*-throw from Michael's dorm and can drop by to visit him there any time he wants (and frequently does so – thank God he has to buzz Michael's room to be let up and can't just come strolling in, or there might have been some awkward moments), and there are plenty of other psychotherapists in the neighbourhood for him to hang out with.

And Lilly says life with her mother is practically unbearable, since Mrs Dr Moscovitz has put them both on low-carb diets and banished bagels from the breakfast table entirely and meets with her trainer like four times a week.

But what about MY share of Michael time? I mean, I am the girlfriend. Even if I am still not prepared to go as far as he might want to go, making-out-wise.

Which is actually a good thing, considering what Mr Dr Moscovitz could have walked in on, that one time.

FtLouie: I didn't mean that literally! I meant maybe we could have a nice dinner, just you and me.
>
SkinnerBx: Oh. Sure. But you can have that any time. I mean, what do you REALLY want?

What DO I really want? World peace, of course. An end to emissions of the greenhouse gases that are causing global warming. For the Drs Moscovitz to get back together so I can see my boyfriend on Friday nights again. To not be a princess any more. To have things go back to the way they used to be, when things were simpler . . . like that time we all went ice-skating at Rockefeller Center and I bit my tongue – only without the tongue-biting part.

And the part where Michael was there with Judith Gershner and I was there with Kenny Showalter.

But you know. Aside from that.

But none of these things is something Michael can actually get me. He has no control over world peace, global warming, his parents, or the fact that they close the skating rink at Rockefeller Center on April 1, so I've never been able to go ice-skating on my birthday.

And he certainly has no control over the fact that I'm a princess. Unfortunately.

FtLouie: Seriously, Michael. Except for a nice dinner, I don't want anything.
>
SkinnerBx: Are you SURE? Because that's not what you said at Christmas.

SWEET SIXTEEN *continues on page 34*

# HOW CONFIDENT ARE YOU, PRINCESS?

## Take this fun quiz to find out!

**1.** **You're planning a party, so you . . .**
   (a) get all your closest mates and a few guys round to your house
   b) hire a huge venue and plan *the* party of the year
   c) what, *you,* throw a party?

**2.** **You're on a bus and your mobile rings. You . . .**
   a) whip it out and start chatting, even though everyone can hear you
   (b) answer it, but speak <u>really</u> quietly
   c) let it go to voicemail

**3.** **You spy a hottie and . . .**
   a) start shaking, then sweating
   b) walk straight up to him and get talking
   (c) catch his eye and smile

**4.** **A popular girl says she thinks your shoes are fab. You . . .**
   a) reply, 'Yeah, I know,' and tell her how much they cost and what size you are . . .
   (b) sheepishly look down at your feet and blush
   c) say, 'Thanks,' and feel chuffed all day

**5.** **In Maths, you think you know the answer to a question. You . . .**
   a) keep quiet – you're probably wrong
   b) quickly shout it out
   (c) put up your hand and hope you get picked

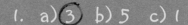

Add up your score and
calculate your confidence rating

1. a) (3) b) 5 c) 1
2. a) 5 b) (3) c) 1
3. a) 1 b) 5 c) (3)
4. a) 5 b) (1) c) 3
5. a) 1 b) 5 c) (3)

If you scored 5–10, you're . . .

## Princess Bashful

You're one shy princess who's lacking in self-confidence. Try saying what you think sometimes: people will respect you for speaking up – even if you're wrong. It's that easy. Honest.

If you scored 11–16, you're . . .

## Princess Confidence

Congratulations, you've got it spot on! You love speaking up but you know when to pipe down too. You've got lots of self-respect and other people value what you have to say.

If you scored 17–25, you're . . .

## Princess Me, me, me

Whoa there! You may love being the centre of attention, but remember: this can come across as a bit arrogant. Why not let your fellow princesses share the spotlight?

# PRINCESS TOP TENS

## Just fill 'em in!

## MY TOP TEN PRINCES
(don't have to be actual princes, just totally hot guys)

1. David Tennant
2. Ian H Watkins
3. Ben Poolman
4. Orlando Bloom
5. Micheal
6. Jhon Barrowman
7. Lee
8. Jack
9. Danny Elfman
10. Daniel Radcliff

## TEN THINGS I'D DO IF I WAS A PRINCESS

1. Ask out David Tennent!
2. Buy 100 ackers of forest.
3. Buy some really cool clothes.
4. Give money to Africa so they can build houses.
5.
6.
7.
8.
9.
10.

## TOP TEN CELEBS
## I'D INVITE TO STAY
## IN MY PALACE
## IF I WAS A PRINCESS

1. ...Billie...Pipper...........
2. ..David...Tennent.........
3. ..H..from..'steps'...........
4. ...Jhon...Barrowman....
5. ...Johnny...................
6. ....Daniel...Radcliff.......
7. ..........................................
8. ..........................................
9. ..........................................
10. .........................................

## MY FAVOURITE
## THINGS

1. Food: ...Pizza!....................
2. Colour: hmm.....Deep purple.
3. Movie: ...................................
4. TV show: ...DR WHO!!...........
5. Actors: David Tennant & ....
   Billie Piper.
6. Actress: ..Billie.P,..Lisa kudrow,
7. Books: Ingo, the deep, Harry Potter
   1,2,3, 4,5,6 & 7, Scorpio, Arkangle
   All american girl 1 & 2, Princess diaries
   etc.
8. Singer: ..................................
9. Song: ..Rule the World by
   take that.
10. Band: ....................................

33

What did I say I wanted at Christmas? I can't even remember now. I hope he's not thinking of getting me another Fiesta Giles action figure. Because now that Buffy's only on in reruns, it just makes me sad to look at her and her friends on their little plastic stands in the cemetery on my dresser. In fact, I've been thinking of replacing them with a lavender plant, since the smell of lavender is supposed to be soothing and I need all the soothing I can get.

Or the Napoleon Dynamite Style Time Machine Modulus Mr Gianini confiscated off a kid in his freshman Algebra class and gave to me. Whichever fits better.

Besides, Michael doesn't have time to be bidding on eBay. He needs to spend what little free time he has with me.

OK, I have to put the kibosh on the gift thing. It's got to be really hard on Michael, figuring out what to get for a girl who can basically get anything she wants from her palace. He's just a poor, hard-working student. It's just not fair on him. Or any boy who might happen to be dating a princess.

```
FtLouie: I have an idea. Let's make a rule: from now on we
can only give each other presents we've MADE.
>
SkinnerBx: Are you serious?
>
FtLouie: Serious as L. Ron Hubbard was that we all have
alien souls trapped inside us.
>
SkinnerBx: OK. You're on.
>
WomynRule: POG, are you online with my brother again?
```

Crud. It's Lilly.

```
FtLouie: Yes. What do you want?
>
WomynRule: Just to remind you that SHE FLEW IN ON A
HELICOPTER.
>
```

FtLouie: I have flown in to tons of things in a helicopter.

Although this is not strictly true. I have only been on a helicopter once, when there was an accident on the FDR and there was no other way to get to the private jet parked at Teterboro.

But I know what Lilly is getting at, and I'm trying to nip it in the bud.

Iluvromance: Mia, you HAVE to have a party. You HAVE to. I know you're upset about what happened at your birthday party last year.

Oh, great! Now Tina's getting in on it too?

FtLouie: Gang up on me, why don't you, everybody.
>
Iluvromance: Lilly PROMISES what happened last year at your party won't happen this year. We won't play Seven Minutes in Heaven. We are way more mature than that now.
>
WomynRule: And besides, I'm with J.P. now.
>
FtLouie: You were with Boris then. But it still happened.
>

WomynRule: But things with Boris were so boring. I mean, where could it go?
>
Iluvromance: Um. Ahem.
>
WomynRule: Sorry. I'm sure things with you and Boris are totally different.
>
Iluvromance: Dang straight.
>

WomynRule: But you know what I mean. Things with J.P. are
still so . . . well . . . you know.

Did we ever. Because Lilly can talk of hardly anything else. I had never seen her
so besotted for a guy. I suppose because J.P. keeps her guessing as to what his real
feelings for her are. It seems like all I ever hear from her these days – when she
isn't going on about her hatred for Andy Milonakis – is, 'Do you think he likes
me? I mean, we go out, and stuff, and we kiss, but he doesn't say stuff, you know,
about how he feels about me. Do you think that's weird? I mean, what kind of guy
doesn't talk about his feelings? Well, OK, I know MOST guys don't talk about
their feelings. But I mean, what guy who goes to AEHS doesn't want to talk about
his feelings? Who isn't gay, I mean?'
   As if I'm supposed to know.

Iluvromance: Has he still not said the L word, Lilly?
>
WomynRule: He hasn't even said the G word. As in, that I'm
his girlfriend.
>
FtLouie: Have YOU said the L word to HIM? Or the B word?
   >
      WomynRule: Of COURSE not. We've only been going out
      for a little over a month. I don't want to scare
      him off.
         >
         FtLouie: Faint heart never won fair lady.
         >
         WomynRule: Stop quoting Gilbert and Sullivan
         at me. I want him to say the L word first. Is
         that such a crime? WHY WON'T HE SAY IT????
            >
         Iluvromance: Well, you know J.P. has always
         been something of a loner. He probably just
         doesn't know how to act around girls.
      >

WomynRule: Do you really think so?

>

FtLouie: Totally. Oh my God, you guys, check it out: J.P.'s like the Beast from Beauty and the Beast, you know, when Belle first comes to live in the palace, and the Beast is all mean to her? Because, just like the Beast was alone in his castle for all those years, J.P. sat by himself at a lunch table for a really long time, so maybe he isn't entirely sure how people are supposed to interact, because he hasn't had all that much experience with human interaction - JUST LIKE THE BEAST!!! So he may come off as gruff or non-emotional, when I'm sure the opposite is true - JUST LIKE THE BEAST!!!!

>

WomynRule: Mia, I know Beauty and the Beast is your favourite musical and all. But I think that's sort of stretching it.

>

Iluvromance: No, I think Mia is right. All J.P. needs is the right woman to unlock his heart - which up until now he has kept in a cold, hard shell for his own emotional protection - and he will be like an unstoppable volcano of passion.

>

WomynRule: In that case why hasn't he exploded already? Unless you're implying I'm not the right woman to unlock his heart.

>

Iluvromance: I'm not saying that! I'm just saying that it won't be easy.

>

FtLouie: Yeah. Like it wasn't easy for Belle to win the Beast's trust.

>

WomynRule: Whatever! It took her like two songs!
>
Iluvromance: Yeah, but real life isn't like a musical.
Unfortunately.
>
FtLouie: Maybe if you said you loved him first, it would
cause the first crack in his hard outer shell . . .
>
WomynRule: I AM NOT SAYING I LOVE HIM FIRST!!!!
>
SkinnerBx: Mia? Are you still there?

My boyfriend! I had got so involved talking about Lilly's boyfriend, I totally forgot
about my own!

FtLouie: Of course I am. Hang on a minute.
>
FtLouie: You guys, I have to go, but one last thing: I AM
NOT HAVING A SWEET-SIXTEEN PARTY AND THAT'S FINAL. GOT IT?
>
WomynRule: God, all right already. You don't have to shout.
>
Iluvromance: Mia, no one wants you to do anything you don't
want to do. But your sweet sixteen IS a big deal . . .
>
FtLouie: NO PARTY.
>
WomynRule: Well, better make sure your grandma knows that
then.
>
FtLouie: Wait. What is THAT supposed to mean?
>
WomynRule: Nothing. I have to go now.
>
FtLouie: LILLY!!! ARE YOU AND GRANDMERE PLOTTING SOMETHING
BEHIND MY BACK AGAIN????

```
>
WomynRule: terminated
>
FtLouie: I'm going to kill her.
>
Iluvromance: She can't help it. You know how upset she's
been since her parents' separation. Not to mention this
Andy Milonakis thing. And the fact that J.P. won't admit
his true feelings for her. Oops, I hear my mom calling. I
have to go. Bye!
>
Iluvromance: terminated
```

Great. Just great.

```
FtLouie: Michael, do you know if your
sister and my grandmother are planning
something for my birthday? Like a
surprise party?
>
SkinnerBx: Not that I'm aware of. Can
you imagine what kind of party those
two would come up with?
```

Actually, I can:

    The kind of party I'd really, really hate.

SWEET SIXTEEN *continues on page 46*

# PARTY PRINCESS

## How to plan a dazzling Princess party!

It can be kind of stressful hosting a party: you have loads of things to plan AND you're required to present a calm, stylish and fun-loving exterior to your guests at all times. This can be difficult to pull off – but not if you check out these tips for the perfect party!

- **ASK PERMISSION.** There is no quicker way to destroy the mood of a swinging party than to have your parents turn up halfway through, furious. Never keep the party a secret. You will be anxious, your guests will sense the tension and your parents WILL find out. And besides, you'll need parental support if you going to make this the party of the year.

- If you're throwing the party in the evening, let your neighbours know in advance. You should also let them know what time you are expecting the party to finish.

- Think about the time and date carefully. Ensure that it doesn't clash with any major events or rival parties.

**Now for the all-exciting details . . .**

# THE GUEST LIST

It is best to approach **guest selection** as you would international peace negotiations. That is the level of tact and forethought we are talking about! Be honest – who would you really like to be there to celebrate with you? And remember, if you haven't invited somebody, don't rub his or her nose in it.

# INVITATIONS

**Individual invitations** set the tone for your gathering. They imply that this will be an exclusive soiree for the elite, not a free-for-all for anyone on the lookout for free cake.
**Personally designed invitations** are always a nice idea. Maybe you could include a comic photo of you as a baby. Just run it through a photocopier with the party details. Or, if you have a digital camera, download the photo and make e-invites.
See CRAFTY PRINCESS on page 66 for other ideas.

# DECORATIONS

**Decoration** is very important if you want to create the right ambience. Fairy lights look pretty and add a bit of party sparkle. Flowers lend an air of sophistication. Try snipping off the stems and float the flower in a dish of water. You can add tea lights too (they float!).

# GAMES

Games can be played with **cool irony**. And they're FUN! How long is it since you played Pass the Parcel or Musical Bumps? Twister is a great **ice-breaker**.

# THEMES

The key to a successful **fancy-dress party** is to ensure that everybody is entering into the spirit of things fully. It has to be all or nothing: state the theme on the invite.
**Colour schemes** can work – (how about Think Pink, Black is Back or Purple Power?) Also try Outrageous 80s, Hats 'n' Wigs or Hollywood Hoedown. Try and match the food and drinks to the theme if possible.

# WHAT TO WEAR

**The belle of the ball** (YOU) must know exactly what she is wearing at least two days before the party. Shoes and accessories should be chosen with care and hair and make-up perfected. Go for a look you know works: that way you'll feel more comfortable.

# FOOD

Party food should be uncomplicated and easy to eat. Guests do not expect a three-course gourmet meal. Try:

- mini pizza slices
- carrot / cucumber / celery sticks to dip in hummus or guacamole
- bowls of nuts and crisps
- decorated fairy cakes
- mini fruit-salad kebabs – an alternative to the cheese-and-pineapple combo. Skewer a grape, a square of melon and a satsuma segment with a cocktail stick.

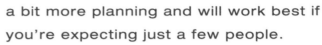

If you're having more of an intimate dinner party, you could try making the food a feature. These suggestions take a bit more planning and will work best if you're expecting just a few people.

- Give each guest their own pizza base. Set some bowls of different ingredients out, including tomato sauce to spread on the base. Then guests construct their own dinner!
- Make a batch of plain fairy cakes. Set out icing pens in various colours. You can all decorate the cakes with your own messages and pictures.
- Make a chocolate fondue. Melt down a big bar of chocolate. Guests stick pieces of fruit on the end of a skewer and dip them in the chocolate. Yum.

# DRINK

- Create your own **punch** recipe by mixing your favourite juices and fruits.
- The day before the party fill some ice-cube trays with fruit juices. Add to lemonade to give it a splash of colour and a hint of fruity flavour.
- See **COCKTAIL PRINCESS** on page 73 for some seriously delicious and impressive mocktails.

# MUSIC

**Crucial element!** If you have an iPod you can make a party playlist of all your favourite tunes. Or if you have access to a CD burner, try making a mix CD. Alternatively, just have your CDs at the ready!

# FINAL PREPARATIONS

Leave yourself plenty of time to shower, get dressed and do your hair and your make-up. Invite your best friends round early so you can all get ready together and get in the party mood.

The **duties** of a hostess are always the same, whatever the occasion.

- See that your guests are comfortable and know where the food and drink are.
- Introduce guests who don't know one another.
- Mingle, mingle, mingle.
- Relax, smile and **have fun!**

## Princess Mia's Christmas Party Tip

Real mistletoe in short supply? Make your own! All you need is

- green felt
- white imitation pearls
- scissors
- glue

Cut out two leaf shapes from the green felt. Glue them together. In the middle of where they are joined, glue several imitation pearls. Let dry. Then hold your fake mistletoe over your head when a cute guy approaches and tell him he has to kiss you.

**It works!**

## Princess Mia's Party Tip

Leave a few disposable cameras around the place. Your guests can pick them up and take pictures throughout the party. You'll end up with photos of everybody and heaps of memories.

## Princess Mia's Anti-Valentine Party!

If you don't have a date, Valentine's Day can suck. So why not get all your single girlfriends round, rent a stack of scary movies and order some tasty take-out? But you all have to make a solemn oath **not** to talk about boys all night.

43

# A-MAZE-ING PRINCESS

Mia has been separated from her one-true-love.
Can you help her find a way out of the maze and
into Michael's arms?

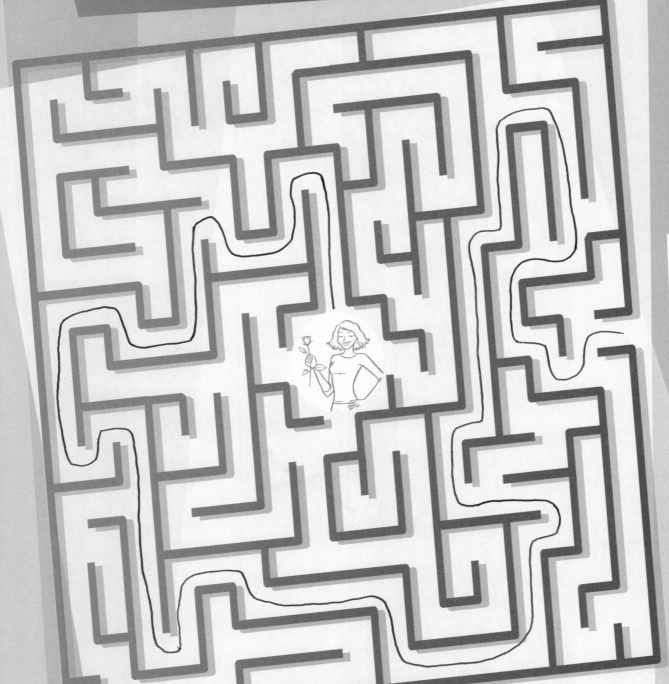

For solution see page 92

# HIDDEN PRINCESS

Can you find all of these THE PRINCESS DIARIES-related
words in the grid below?

Words are hidden horizontally, vertically and diagonally -
and run backwards and forwards!

```
Z M N N C U U H B D H J J A B G R I R Z
P E J L B O R O Y A L D J M L Y Y C U Y
U J S H O X E T E K A J I Z B G C F R M
N E O Y D S V Y B E H Z F A E J E V S W
T C Q D B G O J K E F G Z Z R T N B N Z
S T O O B X L F I M J U S I H Y U C R C
O H M Q G U S P S A E Q I R I A A V Z A
L E S S O N S S C H D C O J R K L K Y Y
C S H F U K C G E S K N N A P P V T U W
N O N G S U T E P C E F I I Q N L I O F
Y Q C K B I G U T T N T Z C R W I Z E F
S E V U O Z H X R B H I J C E P L I F V
H M V X S P Q G E H I M R R I G L N D Q
E L T S A C O A Z P C I I P T G Y I M P
O S F N S R I V U X M I A Q T G M P Z A
U K I X F V T O S G V X Y A O O A Z G V
A J J R O Z I F J N O N Y P H U D N X E
H O T N O Y C A V J G T I B L U K W O G
F C E E X B D T Z K C U K O P I X U O J
D G F A Y Y U W E F W X J A W D K Z Y X
```

| ALGEBRA | FROG | LOVE | ROYAL |
| BOOTS | GENOVIA | MIA | SCEPTRE |
| BORIS | HOTTIE | PAULO | SHAMEEKA |
| CASTLE | LESSONS | PRINCE | THRONE |
| DIARY | LILLY | PRINCESS | TIARA |

45

For solution see page 92

### Thursday, April 29, Homeroom

I asked my mom at breakfast this morning if Grandmere and Lilly were planning a surprise party for my sweet sixteen, and she choked on her fresh-squeezed OJ from Papaya King and went, 'Sweet Jesus, I hope not.'

To which Mr Gianini added, 'Don't expect me to chaperone if they are. I saw enough grinding at the Non-denominational Winter Dance this year to last me a lifetime.'

Which is true. Grinding does seem to be all the rage around Albert Einstein High lately. I wish it was krumping instead. But no. My peers (all except for Michael, who is opposed to grinding for reasons he has yet to share with me, beyond saying it's 'stupid-looking') seem only to want to rub their private parts against one another.

Too bad they won't let us do THAT in PE.

'I thought you didn't want a party this year,' my mom said. 'Because of what happened at your party last year.'

'I don't,' I said. 'But, you know . . . people don't always listen to me.'

By people, of course, I meant Grandmere. As my mom well knew.

'Well, you can rest easy,' my mom said. 'I haven't heard anything about Lilly and your grandmother planning any party.'

I quizzed Lilly at length about my suspicions in the limo on the way to school, but she never once cracked.

Perhaps I was only imagining the whole Grandmere/Lilly plot to fête me against my will.

Which isn't any wonder, really, if you think about all the stuff they've got up to behind my back in the past. Really, they are like the Snape/Malfoy pairing of the Muggle world. Only without the cloaks.

### Thursday, April 29, Gifted and Talented

I observed J.P. closely all through lunch to see if I could detect any signs that he might explode in a volcano of passion, as Tina suggested he was going to some day.

He must have noticed me staring at him though, because at one point when Lilly got up to get a second helping of mac and cheese (her mother's low-carb diet has had the opposite effect she'd evidently hoped for where Lilly is concerned – it has only turned Lilly into even more of a raging carboholic), he looked at me and went, 'Mia. Do I have something on my face?'

I was like, 'No. Why?'

'Because you keep looking at me.'

Busted! How embarrassing!

'Sorry,' I muttered into my Diet Coke, hoping he wouldn't notice how I was blushing. Only how could he not, under the unforgiving glare of the fluorescent overheads? (Note to self: look into cost of getting new, more flattering lighting in caff.) 'I was just . . . checking something.'

'Checking what?'

'Nothing,' I said hastily and dug into my bean salad.

'Mia,' J.P. started to say, in a soft – but deep – voice that (not surprisingly, considering the fact that Boris, across the table, had his violin out, and was showing Tina, Ling Su and Perin how easy it was to pluck out the chords to the Foo Fighters' 'Best of You') only I could hear. 'Do you—'

But he never got to finish whatever it was he was going to say to me, because at that moment Lilly returned.

'Can you believe they were out of mac and cheese?' she asked. 'I had to settle for four slices of bread and a bag of Doritos.' She seemed to overcome her disappointment pretty quickly though, if how fast she chowed down those Doritos is any indication.

I wonder what J.P. was going to say to me?

I think Tina is definitely right. One of these days he's going to blow like Mount Vesuvius. There will be no controlling J.P.'s eruption of passion when it finally happens.

## Thursday, April 29, 7 p.m., Limo Home from the Plaza

I walked into Grandmere's suite at the Plaza only to be attacked by this woman with purple hair in a pair of lowriders who went, 'Oh great, she's here,' and tried to stick a portable microphone pack down the back of my skirt.

'What are you DOING?' I demanded.

Fortunately Lars was with me, and he stepped in front of the woman and said, looking down at her all menacingly, 'May I help you?'

Ms Purple Hair had to crane her neck to see Lars's face. Apparently she didn't like what she saw up there, since she took a few stumbling steps backwards and went, 'Um . . . Lewis? We've got a slight . . . or, I guess I should say, big – really big – problem.'

Which is when this skinny guy in a pair of fancy red glasses came hurrying out of Grandmere's living room, going, 'Oh great, she's here. Princess Mia, I'm so glad to meet you. I'm Lewis, and this is my assistant, Janine –' He indicated the purple-haired woman, who was still staring up at Lars like she was looking at King Kong or someone, and seemed unable to utter a sound. 'If you'd just let Janine put your mic on, we can go ahead and get started.'

I didn't bother asking Lewis what it was we could go ahead and get started. Instead I went, 'Excuse me,' and walked past him and right up to Grandmere, who was sitting in her pink Louis XV chair with her hair all freshly set, her make-up perfect and a trembling, nearly hairless miniature poodle in her lap.

'Oh, Amelia, good, you're here,' she said. 'Where's your mic?'

'Grandmere,' I said, noticing for the first time the cameraman hovering by her shoulder, 'what is going on? Who are these people? Why is that man filming us?'

'He isn't going to be able to use any of the footage, Mia, if you don't put a mic on,' Grandmere said irritably. 'Janine! Janine, would you please put a mic on her?'

Lewis came in, bobbing his spiky-haired head.

'Um, yes, Your Highness, well, Janine tried, see, but there appears to be a problem—'

'What problem?' Grandmere demanded imperiously.

'She, um . . .' Lewis said, looking scared. But not of Lars. Of Grandmere. '. . . wouldn't let Janine put it on her.'

Grandmere swung the evil eye she'd been focusing on Lewis on to me.

'Amelia,' she said coldly. 'Kindly allow the violet-haired young lady to put a microphone on you, so that we can get this out of the way. I have a dinner engagement I don't care to miss.'

'Nobody's putting anything on me,' I said so loudly that Rommel, in Grandmere's lap, put his ears back and whimpered, 'until someone explains to me what's going on.'

'Oh, sorry,' Lewis said, looking mortified. 'I thought you knew. I had no idea. Janine and I – oh, and that's Rafe, with the camera –' Rafe, a burly guy in a bandanna, waved at me from behind his camera lens – 'are from MTV, and you're currently being filmed for a very special episode of MTV's hit reality series *My Super Sweet Sixteen*.'

I looked from Lewis to Grandmere to Rafe – I couldn't see Janine, because she was still out in the foyer with Lars – and back again.

'What?' I said.

'*My Super Sweet Sixteen* is a reality television series on MTV,' Lewis explained, as if that were the part I was having trouble with. 'Each week it features a different teen getting ready to celebrate his or her sixteenth birthday party. We film all the preparations leading up to the party, and then the party itself. It's one of our most popular shows. Surely you've seen it.'

'Oh, I've seen it all right,' I said. 'Which is why I'm out of here. Bye.'

And I started to leave.

BECAUSE I KNEW IT!!!! I KNEW MY GRANDMOTHER HAD BEEN UP TO SOMETHING!!!!!

But I didn't get very far, on account of tripping over a power cord for one of the lights they'd set up.

Also on account of Grandmere standing up (dislodging a very surprised Rommel, who fortunately, due to years of practice, was able to land on his feet) and saying, 'Amelia! Sit down this instant!'

It's her voice. There's just something about that voice that MAKES you do what she says. I don't know how she does it, but she does.

I found myself sinking down on to the couch, nursing the shin I'd bonked against her coffee table.

'That's better,' Grandmere said, in a totally different tone. She sank back down into her fancy pink chair. 'Now, let's try that again. Amelia, these nice people are going to televise your sweet-sixteen birthday party on a special edition of their reality series. This will generate a great deal of publicity for the country of Genovia, over which you will one day rule and which is currently suffering from an almost total lack of American tourists, thanks to the weak dollar and your father's recent decision to limit the number of cruise ships that may dock there to twelve per week. Now, please allow Janine to put a microphone on you so that we can begin. I don't want to keep my dinner date waiting. Mr Castro is a very impatient man.'

I took a deep breath. Then I went – even though I really, really didn't want to know – 'What sweet-sixteen birthday party?'

'The one I am throwing for you,' Grandmere said. 'I shall be flying you and one hundred of your closest friends in the royal jet to Genovia, where you'll be met at the airport by horse-drawn carriages and taken immediately to the palace for a champagne brunch, followed by an all-expenses-paid shopping trip to boutiques such as Chanel and Louis Vuitton on the Rue de Prince Phillipe for the girls and a trip to the Genovian beach for private jet-ski lessons for the boys. Then it's back to the palace for massages and fashion and beauty makeovers. Then everyone is invited to a black-tie ball in your honour, at which Destiny's Child, who have agreed to reunite for one night only and on your behalf, will perform their greatest hits. After which I will have everyone flown home the following morning so that they arrive back in America in time for school on Monday.'

I could only stare at her. I knew my mouth was open. I also knew that Rafe was filming the whole thing.

But I couldn't close my mouth. And I couldn't summon the words to ask Rafe to put his camera down.

Because I was totally FREAKED!!!!

Champagne brunches? All-expenses-paid shopping trips to Louis Vuitton? Massages? Destiny's Child? One hundred of my closest friends?

I don't even KNOW one hundred people, much less have that many friends.

'It's going to be spectacular,' Lewis said, pulling up a chair so he could peer at me more closely through the lenses of his red-framed glasses – which kind of resembled plastic scissor handles, I noticed. 'It'll be the most fantastic episode of *My Super Sweet Sixteen* ever. We're even changing the name of the programme just for your episode . . . we're calling it *My Super ROYAL Sweet Sixteen*. Your party, Princess, is going to make every other party ever featured on this show look like a five-year-old's birthday party at Chuck E. Cheese.'

'And,' Grandmere said – up close, I could see that she had really layered on the pancake make-up for the benefit of the camera – 'it will attract millions of eager tourists to Genovia, once they've seen all that our little country has to offer by way of exclusive, high-end shopping, world-class entertainment, seaside recreation opportunities, fine dining, luxury accommodation and old-world hospitality.'

I looked from Grandmere to Lewis and then back again, my mouth still open.

Then I jumped up and ran for the door.

## Thursday, April 29, the Loft

Well, who wouldn't have run? This has got to be, hands down, the most disturbing thing she's ever done. Seriously. I mean, MTV? *My Super ROYAL Sweet Sixteen*? Has she lost her mind?

She called Mom to complain, of course. About me. She says I'm being selfish and ungrateful. She says all I ever think about is myself, and that this is a tremendous opportunity for Genovia to finally get some good press after all the negative news stories about it lately, considering the snail thing and almost getting thrown out of the EU, and all. She says if I really cared about the country over which I will some day rule, I would accept her generous gift and agree to be filmed doing so.

And I DO really care about Genovia. I DO.

BUT I DO NOT WANT A SWEET-SIXTEEN BIRTHDAY PARTY!!!!!

And I particularly do not want one that is going to be BROADCAST AROUND THE COUNTRY ON MTV!!!!!!!

Why is that so hard for people to understand????

At least Mom's on my side. When she heard what Grandmere (and MTV) had planned, her lips got all small, the way they do when she's really, really mad. Then she said, 'Don't worry, honey. I'll take care of it.'

Then she went to make some phone calls.

To my dad in Genovia, I hope. Or possibly to an insane asylum, so that Grandmere can be locked up at last for her own – and my – protection.

But I suppose that's a little too much to ask.

Why can't I have a NORMAL grandma? One who'd make me a cake for my birthday, instead of hosting a transcontinental royal slumber party for me and allowing a cable network to FILM it?

WHY?

SWEET SIXTEEN *continues on page 58*

# WHICH PRINCESS ARE YOU?

Answer the questions below to discover your princess match!

**1. What is your dream job?**
- a) Anything that involves helping other people.
- b) Actress
- (c) Writer
- d) World leader, of course!

**2. What is your personal style?**
- (a) Unique, hard to categorize
- b) Classic and chic
- c) Feminine but funky
- d) Glamorous

**3. What quality do you find most attractive in a guy?**
- (a) Sense of humour
- b) Sophistication
- c) Thoughtfulness
- d) Ambition

**4. Which of these words best describes you?**
- a) Funny
- b) Charming
- c) Loyal
- (d) Feisty

**5. Which of the following could you not live without?**
- (a) Books
- b) Make-up
- c) Music
- d) Boys!

**6. What would be your ideal home?**
- a) Cool loft apartment in the city
- (b) Luxury villa by the sea
- c) Fabulous castle
- d) Mansion with tennis courts and lots of staff

**7. What is your favourite kind of film?**
- (a) Comedy
- b) Drama
- c) Romantic
- d) Action

**If you answered mostly a, you are Princess Mia.**

You are the kind of princess who feels more comfortable in jeans than a gown – but you look amazing in both! Just like Princess Mia, you are smart and romantic – and you think it's every princess's duty to make the world a better place.

**If you answered mostly b, you are Princess Grace of Monaco.**

Hello, Princess Hollywood! Grace Kelly was a truly beautiful actress in the 1950s and was rich and famous in her own right before she met Prince Rainier and became a princess. The people of Monaco loved Princess Grace and, like her, you know how to make other people feel like they really matter. Plus you can really work those giant A-list sunglasses!

**If you answered mostly c, you are Princess Beauty.**

A real-life fairytale princess, just like beauty from *Beauty and the Beast*, you're beautiful inside and out! You're also the perfect princess to have around in a crisis. Beauty found her handsome prince in the most unexpected place – and you totally believe in the power of love too! Aw.

**If you answered mostly d, you are Princess Cleopatra.**

Just like Cleo – last of the Egyptian monarchs – you were born to rule! You're very clever and you know how to get what you want. Princess Cleo once arrived at Julius Caesar's house rolled up in a carpet, from which she was dramatically unrolled by her attendants; you too love being the centre of attention – especially when there's a hottie around!

# ECO-PRINCESS!

## Rule the world and save the planet
### By Princess Mia

Every princess has a responsibility to protect the environment for the populace and the future populace. I want to make sure this planet and all the species on it stick around for a while. So what can YOU do to help . . . ?

Princesses Don't Litter. Ever. *except in life threatening situations*
There is always a bin nearby, so use it! If you have to chew gum, always wrap it up and put it in the bin. NEVER spit it out on to the street. *Except in Life threatening situations.*

Recycle.
It isn't hard. If your parents aren't recycling, check out the schemes in your area. Magazines, plastics, cans, glass and clothing are usually all good to go.

Cars are BAD for the environment. They emit nasty fumes and they use up heaps of our vital resources. If you get a lift to school, why not walk or ride a bike? Alternatively, take public transport – more environmentally friendly than everyone driving around in their own car. And a good way to mingle with your public.

. . . yadda yadda yadda . . .

Don't leave your television / iPod / private jet on standby, or your mobile phone charger plugged in, because it is a TOTAL WASTE of energy.

? A

I KNOW!!

Conserve energy by switching off the lights when you leave a room. Remember, there's no one in there

one step ahead of you mate

Use long-life bulbs in all your chandeliers.

I alread do.

Don't ever eat tuna that isn't dolphin-friendly. Remember, dolphins are our friends.

tuna? - yuk!!!

If you're only wearing a T-shirt, you could always put a jumper on instead of turning up the central heating . . . Conserve energy!

I am always cold so watever.

Have a shower instead of a bath. It uses much less water so is eco-friendly. Obviously all princesses need a good long soak sometimes – just not every day.

How eco friendy am I? I don't even have a shower.

Support candidates who want to protect the environment. Even if you're too young to vote, you can volunteer to help candidates who are working to make the air safe for all of us to breathe. Plus you can have fundraisers for green organizations like Greenpeace and Friends of the Earth.

gottcha

**1.** Unscramble the letters to reveal *The Princess Diaries* characters!

A BAHAMA NIB KIT

..............................

TAN AS BOISE

..............................

A PRINCE MISS

..............................

ERRAND MEG

Grandmere

..............................

AM CHILE

Michael

..............................

56

**2.** All princesses love to party!
But these party essentials are all mixed up.
Can you solve the anagrams?

ASGME

TSIGF

RYTBHADI

ROECTDANIOS

EMTEH

UCIMS

IVAINOSTINT

2. GAMES, GIFTS, BIRTHDAY, DECORATIONS, THEME, MUSIC, INVITATIONS

### Friday, April 30, Lunch

I was regaling everyone at lunch about Grandmere's crazy scheme – I had purposefully not told anyone about it, including Lilly, just so I could tell everyone about it at the same time, because ever since J.P. started sitting with us at lunch, there's sort of been this contest between us girls to see who can make him laugh the hardest, because, well, J.P. seems like he could use a laugh, being a bottled-up volcano of passion, and all.

Not that anyone has really ADMITTED that's what we do. Try to see who can make J.P. laugh the hardest, I mean.

But we totally do.

At least, I do.

Anyway, I was telling everyone about Lewis, with the scissor-handle glasses, and Janine-of-the-purple-hair, and they were laughing – especially J.P., particularly when I got to the part about the sex-segregated shopping for girls and jet-skiing for boys – when Lilly put down her chicken parm on a roll and was like, 'Frankly, Mia, I think it was extremely uncool of you to turn down your grandmother's generous offer to throw you such a fantastic party.'

I just stared at her with my mouth open, the way I'd stared at Grandmere and Lewis the night before.

'I do think it would be kind of neat to fly to Genovia for the weekend,' Perin said softly from the other side of the table.

'I could totally use a Louis Vuitton violin case,' Boris said.

'But only the girls were allowed to shop,' I pointed out to him. 'You'd have to be jet-skiing with the boys. And you know how you get that allergic reaction to sand-flea bites.'

'Yeah,' Boris grumbled. 'But Tina could have bought one for me.'

'You guys,' I said. I couldn't believe what I was hearing. 'Hello. Have you ever even seen that show, *My Super Sweet Sixteen*? They totally try to make the people on it look bad! On purpose. That's the POINT of the series.'

'Not necessarily,' Lilly said. 'I think the point of the series is to show how some American young people choose to celebrate their coming of age – which in this country is at sixteen – and to convey to audiences what a difficult and yet joyous time it can be, as sweet sixteens struggle on the threshold of adulthood, not quite a child any more, not yet a man or woman. . . .'

Everyone stared at her. J.P. was the one who finally said, 'Um, I always thought the point of the series was to show stupid people spending way too much money on something that ultimately has no meaning.'

'TOTALLY!' I burst out. I couldn't believe J.P. had put it so exactly right. Well, I could, of course, because J.P. is a wordsmith, like me, and aspires to a literary career of some sort, just like I do.

But I also couldn't because, well, he's a guy, and most of the time guys just don't GET stuff like that.

'Lilly,' I said, 'don't you remember that episode where those girls invited five hundred of their closest friends to that rock concert they gave for themselves at that nightclub, and they made that big deal out of not letting freshmen come and had the ones who crashed thrown out by bouncers? Oh, and charged their friends admission to get in? To their own birthday party?'

'And then gave the money to charity,' Lilly pointed out.

'But still!' I said. 'What about that girl who had herself carried into her party on a bed held on the shoulders of eight guys from the local crew team, then forced all her friends to watch a fashion show with herself as the only model?'

'No one is saying you have to do any of those things, Mia.' Lilly glowered.

'Lilly, that's not the point. Think about it,' I said. 'I'm the Princess of Genovia. I'm supposed to be a role model. I support causes like Greenpeace and Homes for the Hopeful. What kind of role model will I be if I show up on TV, spending all that money, flying my friends to Genovia and having a huge shopping spree and rock concert, just for them?'

'The kind who really appreciates her friends,' Lilly said, 'and wants to do something nice for them.'

'I do really appreciate you guys,' I said, a little bit hurt by this. 'And I definitely think each and every one of you deserves a trip to Genovia for shopping sprees and free concerts. But think about it. How's it going to look, spending all that money on a birthday party?'

'It's going to look like your grandmother really, really loves you,' Lilly said.

'No it's not. It's going to look like I'm the biggest selfish spoiled brat on the planet. And if my grandmother really, really loved me,' I said, 'she'd spend all that money on something I really wanted – like helping to feed AIDS orphans in Africa, or even . . . I don't know. Getting stationary bikes for spinning classes at AEHS! – not something I don't care about at all.'

'Mia's right,' Tina said. 'Although . . . I've always wanted to see Destiny's Child in concert.'

'And I've always wanted to see the art collection at the Genovian palace,' said Ling Su a little wistfully.

'I could totally use a makeover,' Perin said. 'Maybe then people would stop thinking I'm a boy.'

'You guys!' I was shocked. 'You can't be serious! You'd want to let yourselves be filmed doing all that stuff? And have it be shown on MTV?'

Tina, Ling Su, Perin and Boris looked at one another. Then they looked at me and shrugged. 'Yeah.'

'Admit it, Mia,' Lilly said angrily. 'This doesn't have anything to do with you being afraid of looking selfish on TV. It has to do with you still holding what happened at your party last year against me.' Lilly's lips got as small as – maybe even smaller than – my mom's had the night before. 'And so you're going to make everybody here suffer for it.'

Silence roared across the lunch table after Lilly dropped this little bombshell. Boris suddenly didn't seem to know where to look and so settled for staring at the leftover buffalo bites on his tray. Tina turned red and reached for her Diet Coke, sucking very noisily on the straw sticking out of it.

Or maybe her sucking just seemed noisy compared to how quiet everyone had gone.

Except of course for J.P., who, out of everyone there, was the only person who had no idea what Lilly had done at my fifteenth birthday party. Even Perin knew, having been filled in about it by Shameeka during a particularly boring French class. In French, no less.

'Wait,' J.P. said. 'What happened at Mia's party last year?'

'Something,' Lilly said fiercely, her eyes very bright behind her contacts, 'that's never going to happen again.'

'OK,' J.P. said. 'But what was it? And why does Mia still hold it against you?'

But Lilly didn't say anything. Instead she scooted her chair back and ran – pretty melodramatically, if you ask me – to the ladies' room.

I didn't go after her. Neither did Tina. Instead Ling Su did, saying, with a sigh, 'I guess it's my turn anyway.'

The bell rang right after that. As we were picking up our trays to take them back, J.P. turned to me and asked, 'So are you ever going to tell me what that was all about?'

But, remembering what Tina had said about the volcano of passion, I shook my head. Because I don't want him exploding all over ME.


## Friday, April 30, between Lunch and Gifted and Talented

At least Michael is on my side about it. The party thing, I mean. Because when I called him just now on my cell (even though technically this was not an emergency) to tell him what Grandmere had planned, he said, 'When you say transcontinental slumber party, do you mean that we'd get to sleep in the same room?'

To which I replied, 'Most assuredly not.'

'And you haven't changed your mind about having sex with me now?' Michael asked, 'as opposed to after your senior prom?'

'I think you would have been the first to know if I had,' I said, blushing deeply, as I always do when this topic comes up.

'Oh,' Michael said. 'Well, then I'm on your side.'

'But, Michael,' I said, just to make sure I understood. Communication between couples is so important, as we all know from Dr Phil. 'Don't you want to go jet-skiing and see Destiny's Child?'

SWEET SIXTEEN *continues on page 68*

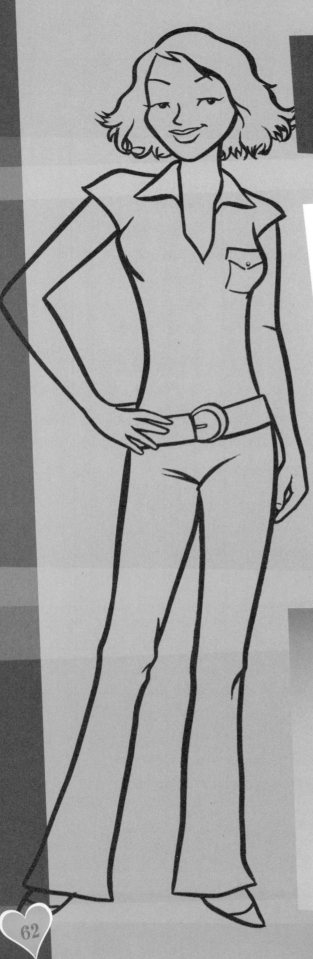

# FASHION PRINCESS

### A Note from Princess Mia

Sad but true: people will totally judge you by what you wear. So you want to look good, but still show your special uniqueness and own individual brand of style.

People who don't have to dress up every time they go out (like I do) are lucky. Still, even if you're only going to school or to the movies, you should try to look cool, while still being comfortable.

## Fashion Tips

- **Magazines** are perfect for fashion tips and trends, but a princess doesn't wear something just because a fashionista tells her to: Mia loves her Dr. Martens boots because they're part of her unique style.

- **Show off** your princess pins with a cute mini or funky shorts, but team them with thick tights for a less in-your-face look!

- **Accessorizing** is a great way to express your personal style. There are some universal no-nos – like wearing a necklace OVER a polo neck or wearing sunglasses indoors – but, on the whole, anything goes. Statement pieces are good: like a pair of brightly coloured, funky shoes worn with a pared-down jeans-and-top outfit, or a chunky beaded necklace worn over a plain, cute T.

- Give unusual **layering** a go. Try wearing the vest tops you usually wear underneath, *over* other tops. Also, shirts can look cool under a T-shirt with the collar showing. Give summer dresses a new lease of life by wearing them over jeans, with a cute cardie to keep you snug.

## Jeans with everything!

Princesses know that denim works for every occasion. Here are a few pointers to help you find your perfect match:

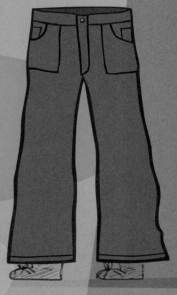

### Boyish

Seriously cute. If you wear boyish jeans with a more girly top the contrast totally works. Also look effortlessly cool with a plain vest top: just add a tiara and some Converse and you're done! Great with flip-flops in the summer.

### Skinny

A total revelation: skinny jeans are surprisingly flattering, even if you're not super-skinny! These look great with flat pumps and under boots – not so good with trainers or heels. Wear under a mini-dress for a totally rocking look.

### ✳ FAVOURITE ✳ Bootleg

The jean-shape that just won't go away – because bootlegs make every princess look so hot! Wear with a dressy top for parties (Princess Cameron Diaz wears hers to premieres all the time). Also look awesome with heels and, um, boots!

### Cropped

Best worn in summer, cropped jeans are laid-back and suit most body shapes. The only rule here is do NOT wear with socks or you will be a royal fashion disaster.

# PRINCESS STYLE
## by Sebastiano

So you want to look like a mod*?
Good for you! What ev* girl needs for
her ward* is this:

- One pair good fit jeans , blue
- One paid good fit jeans, black
- One pair good fit trousers, any colour
- Two sweat*, any colour
- Two blouse, any colour
- T-shirts, many colours
- One skirt, above the knee
  (but not too much)
- One skirt, below the knee
  (but above ankle)

- Socks, any colours
- Tights
- Bras, under*
- One pair smart shoes, low heel
- One pair trainers
- One pair smart shoes, higher heel
- One pair boots, knee-high
- One jack*
- One black coat, knee-length

You should be able to put togeth* a doz* or so great looks. Mix and match! Use your imag*! Borrow your moth's* scarves and necklaces! Wear them wrapped around your head! Who cares what peop* say? Experiment with fash* is only way to know what look is best for you. Only please, for Sebastiano's sake, no princess would ever wear:

ew    - too short miniskirt
ew    - tube top
ew    - too short shorts
ewx2 - thigh-high boots
ew    - stilettos
ew    - fishnets
ew x2 - anything fuschia.

Because English is not Sebastiano's first language, he has some difficulty remembering the endings of many English words e.g. mod* means model.
*Every       *Dozen
*Sweaters    *Mother's
*Jacket      *Fashion
*Wardrobe    *Imagination
*Underwear   *People
*Together

# CRAFTY PRINCESS

**Be a super-creative princess and make your own greetings cards and gift wrap!**

## CARDS

All you need is a blank card (available in art shops) and you're ready to get inspired!

- Choose a design that is appropriate for the person you are giving it to. Try: hearts – stars – a tiara – a lipstick mark – shoes – a handbag – a cat – a cake – candles – butterflies.

- Draw out a plan of your design on a piece of paper first – you can keep referring to this once you start making the card.

- Cut out your design, then arrange your layout to make sure the colours and shapes work together. If you're using fabric you can make a paper template first to get exactly the shape you want.

- Decide how you're going to attach the various elements of your card – you could use a simple running stitch, glue, double-sided tape, or even staples can look funky. Think creatively!

- Try drawing your image on the card and then tracing over it with a thin line of glue. Now sprinkle on glitter or hundreds and thousands, leave for a minute, then shake off. *Voilà!*

## TIPS

- Collect any interesting scraps of fabric, bits of ribbon, beads, sequins and gift wrap from birthdays and Christmas . . . you might come up with some unexpected but cool combinations!

- When using glue, try applying with the end of pen that's run out. This will help you to be precise.

- Always be on the lookout for interesting art supplies. You don't have to be conventional! Try using cake decorations, text cut out from magazines, your favourite sweets . . . whatever catches your eye.

## WRAP IT!

This is a really simple way to make stylish wrapping paper. It works best on rectangular and square gifts.

- Wrap up the present in brown parcel paper.

- Use a fine-liner or gel pen to draw a line all the way round the paper. Draw one line from top to bottom and another from side to side. Make sure you join up the end of the line to the beginning.

- Where the lines cross each other on the front of your present, draw a simple bow. If you like you could draw the outline of a gift tag and write a message in it. You're done!

'Jet-skis are really harmful to the environment, being far more polluting than other two-stroke motors, not to mention that marine mammal experts have testified that personal-watercraft activity near seals, sea lions, and elephant seals disturbs normal rest and social interaction and causes stampedes into the water that can separate seal pups from adult mothers,' Michael said. 'And, no offence, but Destiny's Child is a girl band.'

'Michael,' I said, shocked, 'don't be sexist!'

'I'm not saying they aren't immensely talented, not to mention sexy as hell,' Michael said. 'But let's face it: only girls like to listen to them.'

'I guess you're right,' I admitted.

'But you should let the people who love you throw some kind of party for you,' Michael said. 'Not necessarily on MTV, but you know . . . something. Turning sixteen is a big deal. And it's not like you had a bat mitzvah or anything.'

'But—'

'I know you're still emotionally scarred by what my sister did at your last party,' Michael said, 'but maybe you should give her another chance. After all, she seems totally crazy about J.P. I highly doubt she's going to cheat on him in a closet with a Nepalese busboy.'

'I think Jangbu was Tibetan,' I said.

'Whatever. The point is, Mia, your sweet sixteen should be a birthday you'll remember for all time. It should be special. Don't let Lilly – or your grandmother – dictate how you celebrate it. But DO celebrate it.'

'Thanks, Michael,' I said, feeling truly moved by his words. He is so wise sometimes.

'And if you change your mind about the sex thing,' he joked, 'call me.'

And other times, so not.

### Friday, April 30, Gifted and Talented

I think I finally get it. What's going on with Lilly and this *My Super Royal Sweet Sixteen* thing, I mean.

I figured it out when Lilly looked up from the issue of the '*Zine* – the school literary magazine – she is currently working on and said, in an effort to get me to change my mind about the birthday thing, 'It may be the only way some of us are ever going to get on MTV!'

And then it all became clear. Why it is that Lilly is so adamant about my letting Grandmere go ahead with her birthday plan, I mean.

Think about it. Where on earth would GRANDMERE have got the idea to go on *My Super Sweet Sixteen*? She's never seen that show. She doesn't even know what MTV is. Somebody had to have planted that idea in her head.

And I'm betting that somebody is called Lilly Moscovitz.

I KNEW IT!!!! I KNEW THEY WERE IN ON SOMETHING TOGETHER!!!!

They really ARE like Snape and Malfoy. Minus the cloaks.

'Lilly,' I said, trying to sound understanding and not accusatory. Because Dr Phil says this is the best way to handle conflict resolution. 'I'm sorry Andy Milonakis got his own show and you didn't. And I do think it's a travesty of justice, because your show is way more intelligent AND entertaining than his is. And I'm sorry your parents are separated, and I'm sorry your boyfriend won't say the L-word. But I am not violating my most sacred principles just so that you can finally reach your target demographic. I'm sorry, but there's not going to be any *My Super ROYAL Sweet Sixteen* slumber party in Genovia. And that's final. And you can tell my grandmother that.'

Lilly blinked a few times. 'Me? Tell your grandmother? Why would I tell your grandmother anything?'

'Oh, please,' I said. 'Like you weren't the one who put the bug in her ear about the show *My Super Sweet Sixteen*.'

'Is that what you think?' Lilly demanded, throwing down the pen she was using to mark up *'Zine* submissions. 'Well, what if I did? SOMEONE should do something for your birthday, since you're so opposed to anyone so much as mentioning it.'

'And whose fault is that?' I asked her. 'After you ruined my birthday party last year – not to mention what you did at Christmas, in Genovia—'

'I SAID I WAS SORRY FOR THAT!' Lilly shrieked. 'WHAT DO I HAVE TO DO TO MAKE YOU FREAKING TRUST ME THAT IT WON'T HAPPEN AGAIN?'

'Prove it,' I said, my voice sounding very quiet compared to hers. Which, considering that she was yelling her head off, was kind of no surprise. Lucky for her,

Mrs Hill was in the Teachers' Lounge, calling Visa to get her credit limit extended.

'And how am I supposed to do that?' Lilly wanted to know.

I thought about it. What COULD Lilly do to prove that she would never again betray my trust by making out with (or playing strip bowling with) relative strangers at some party I, or one of my family members, was hosting?

I thought about making her sing 'Don't Cha' ('Don't cha wish your girlfriend was hot like me?') at the next pep rally, in front of the whole school. That would certainly have been entertaining, not to mention interesting, considering how Principal Gupta might react.

But then I thought of something that would be even MORE interesting.

'Tell J.P. that you love him,' I said.

I had the satisfaction of seeing all the blood drain from Lilly's face.

'Mia,' she breathed, 'I can't. You know I can't. We all agreed – boys like to make the first move. They don't like it when girls say the L-word first. They run from them . . . like startled fawns.'

I felt a little twinge of guilt. Because she was right. What I was asking her to do might very well cause J.P. to drop her like a hot potato.

But it was like there was some kind of crazy little mean elf inside me, making me say it anyway.

'Don't you think you're underestimating J.P.?' I asked. 'I mean, he is not like a typical boy. Does a typical boy know the score to *Avenue Q* by heart? Who isn't gay, I mean?'

'No,' Lilly said hesitantly.

'Does a typical boy write poems about the school administration and his desire to bring it down?'

'Um . . .' Lilly said, 'I guess not.'

'And does a typical boy pick all the corn out of his chilli?'

'OK,' Lilly said. 'Granted, J.P. is not a typical boy. But, Mia, what you're asking me to do . . . tell him that I love him . . . it could permanently damage – or end – my relationship with him.'

'Or,' I said, 'it could unloose the lava flow of passion that you and I both know is bubbling just underneath the surface of J.P.'s cool exterior.'

Lilly blinked at me. 'Have you been reading some of Tina's romance novels?' she wanted to know.

I ignored that. Or the little mean elf did.

'If you really and truly want me to forgive you for all those times you ruined my parties,' I said, 'you will tell J.P. you love him.'

Even as the words were coming out of my mouth, I couldn't believe I was saying them. I don't even know why I was saying them. What did I care whether or not Lilly told J.P. she loved him?

Although it would definitely cut down on her whining about his not using the L-word. And I was kind of interested to see what he'd do in response. You know, in a fun, social-experiment kind of way.

Lilly didn't look like she agreed with me though. About it being a fun social experiment to tell J.P. she loved him. In fact, she kind of looked like she wanted to barf.

Which prompted me to ask, 'You do love him, don't you? I mean, you've only been going on about how great he is for the past month and a half.'

'Of course I love him,' Lilly said. 'I'm crazy about him. Who wouldn't be? He's, like, the world's most perfect guy – smart, funny, sensitive, hot, tall, not gay and yet still obsessed with *Wicked*, *The OC*, and *Gilmore Girls*. . . . That's why I don't want to ruin it – what I have with him!'

Which was when I heard myself say, 'It's the only thing I want for my birthday. Besides world peace. Your telling J.P. that you love him, I mean.'

What was WRONG with me? That wasn't ME talking. It was the little mean elf inside my mouth, making it move and say things I didn't actually mean.

Maybe this is what happens when you turn sixteen. A little mean elf moves inside your body and starts controlling your words and actions. Funny how they've never mentioned anything about THAT on *My Super Sweet Sixteen*. Or on *Dr. Phil*.

'This is just like when Henry the Second asked his knights to kill the Archbishop of Canterbury,' Lilly said in a small voice.

'Or when Rachel asked Ross to drink the glass of leftover fat in order to prove his love on *Friends*,' I said. Because I wasn't talking about murdering J.P., for crying out loud.

But was Lilly going to drink the fat?

That was the question she seemed to be struggling with as she murmured, 'I have to go to the office to get something photocopied,' and wandered from the G and T room in a sort of daze.

'Mia,' Boris – who had just been headed into the supply closet to practise his latest piece when Lilly and I had started fighting, and so of course he'd stopped to watch (though he'd pretended to be listening to his iPod) – said, 'What are you doing?'

Even though Boris is already sixteen, he apparently hasn't met his little mean elf. Maybe boys don't get them when they turn sixteen.

Still, I can't say I appreciated his tone. I mean, he knows from first-hand experience how difficult Lilly can be to deal with sometimes.

Really, Lilly should be grateful he hasn't said anything to J.P. about the details surrounding their break-up. I don't think even the Beast would have appreciated hearing about how Belle played Seven Minutes in Heaven with a guy who wasn't her boyfriend right in front of said boyfriend.

I'm just saying.

SWEET SIXTEEN *continues on page 78*

# COCKTAIL PRINCESS

Every royal celebration needs mocktails! Try these delicious concoctions.

## Cinderella Twist

45 ml orange juice
45 ml pineapple juice
15 ml lemon juice
Ice cubes

Pour the juices into a cocktail shaker. Add a scoop of ice, shake vigorously, then strain into a martini glass. Yum.

## Purple Prince

125 ml blueberry juice
15 ml lemon juice
125 ml lemonade
Ice cubes

Place some ice in a medium glass. Add the juices, then stir in the lemonade.

## Tiaratini

serves 2

150 g fresh strawberries or raspberries, or a mixture of both 125 ml cranberry juice

Place the berries in a blender with the juice and whiz until smooth. Pour into martini glasses.

## Princess Colada

125 ml coconut milk
125 ml pineapple juice
5 ice cubes

Blend all the ingredients until smooth. Pour into a long glass.

# PRINCESS *Vain* or PRINCESS Plain?

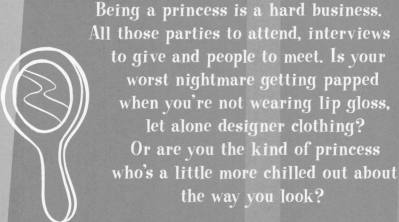

Being a princess is a hard business. All those parties to attend, interviews to give and people to meet. Is your worst nightmare getting papped when you're not wearing lip gloss, let alone designer clothing?
Or are you the kind of princess who's a little more chilled out about the way you look?

Answer the questions and make a note of the points you score (in brackets).

**1.** You're just hanging out, watching TV, when your dad asks you to nip to the shop and get a paper. Before leaving the house . . .

* You iron your fave jeans, spend half an hour carefully applying your make-up — who knows who you might see? — and run the straighteners quickly through your hair. (15)

* To complete your baggy jumper and jeans outfit you slip your trainers on and scrape your hair into a high ponytail. (5)

* It's only a five-minute walk and there's no chance of meeting Orlando Bloom, but a little mascara never hurt anyone! (10)

**2.** You're about to go on holiday. All you'll be able to see from your hotel window will be miles and miles of beach. How do you prepare?

* You're really disorganized and didn't get round to buying any new holiday clothes, so it's last year's bikini and off-white vests for you. You're going to spend most of time in the sea anyway, so who cares? (5)

* You take a good magazine, a great pair of shades and a selection of the very latest bikinis. There's no rescuing the hair once it's been in the sea, so the sun lounger is where you're staying! (15)

* You buy a new bikini, of course, but that's as far as it goes. You always try to pull off the whole natural-beach-beauty thing — it's fine you look great with a tan! (10)

**3.** It's your birthday and your great-auntie and your other generous relatives have finally given up trying to guess what you wear and have sent you cash. It's time to hit the shops. You buy:

* Some thank-you cards and some hair bobbles.(5)

* Another gorgeous dress with a designer tag. (15)

* Some funky jeans and a cool top. (10)

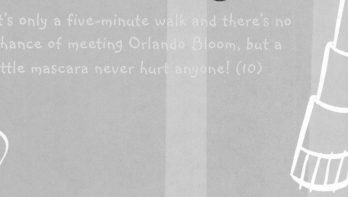

74

**4.** It's your best mate's birthday party. Absolutely everyone that's anyone is going to be there, including the school hottie. How long does it take you to get ready?

\* After make-up, nails, hair, a few changes of outfit and obviously time to dance around in your bedroom – probably about an hour. (10)

\* Well, being that it's a special occasion, you'll have a shower before you go out, but generally you can never be bothered to make a particular effort – erm . . . five minutes? (5)

\* As long as it takes. You're not going to go out looking less than perfect, are you? If every girl there is going to be after one guy, this princess is going to stand out! (15)

**5.** Even princesses get spots (usually the night before your date with Prince Charming). A zit on your face means:

\* Time to get out the ole spot cream, and bug your mum for other miracle remedies. If all else fails, you have concealer. (10)

\* Everyone gets spots, and who are you trying to impress anyway, so what's the big deal? Make-up and squeezing only make it worse. (5)

\* You don't leave the house. You stay in your room, or preferably the cellar, where no one can find you, until it goes. (15)

### If you scored 0-25, you are Princess Plain

Well, clothes and beauty really are a bit too much effort for you, aren't they? That's OK, fashion isn't for everybody, but sometimes there really is no excuse for not taking some time over your appearance. Who knows – you might learn to love a slick of mascara if you gave it a chance!

### → If you scored 30-50, you are Princess Perfect   Yay!!

You have the mix just about right. You don't worship your lipstick, or your high heels, but you understand that on certain occasions they occupy a prime place in your life, and there's absolutely nothing wrong with that!

### If you scored 55-75, you are Princess Vain

Wow – you really are obsessed. Every princess knows the value of making an effort, but there is a limit. Perhaps you need to find it. It lies somewhere around understanding that Yves Saint Laurent make-up isn't always a necessity but that clean hair is.

# ZODIAC PRINCESS

by Princess Mia

## PRINCESS AQUARIUS

(21 January - 19 February)
Changeable, talented, inquisitive.
Does your monarchy need
royal adjustment? You're a
reformer, Aquarius,
so get going!
Best royal consorts:
Gemini, Libra
Possible prince:
Aries, Sagittarius

## PRINCESS PISCES

(20 February - 20 March)
Just like Grandmere.
Sensitive, romantic,
self-sacrificing.
You always do what you
can to help, Pisces, whether it's
political support or a nail file.
Best royal consorts: Cancer, Scorpio
Possible prince: Taurus, Capricorn

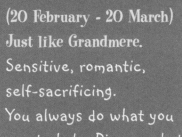

## PRINCESS ARIES

(21 March - 20 April)
Responsible, dynamic, dominant.
If you lead, Aries, the people will follow.
Lead them to wise choices,
fashion included.
Best royal consorts:
Leo, Sagittarius
Possible prince:
Gemini, Aquarius

## PRINCESS TAURUS

(April 21 - May 21) That's me!
Productive, tolerant, patient.
It isn't easy running a kingdom, Taurus, but
nobody vanquishes bureaucracy like you!
Best royal consorts:
Virgo, Capricorn
Possible prince:
Cancer, Pisces

## PRINCESS GEMINI

(May 22 - June 21)
Clever, charming,
flexible.
Gemini, you're extra
easy to work with on matters of state
— you're smart and versatile!
Best royal consorts: Libra, Aquarius
Possible prince: Aries, Leo

## PRINCESS CANCER

(June 22 - July 23)
Intuitive, imaginative, magnetic.
Royal flattery doesn't fool you, Cancer –
you know who your court allies are.
Best royal consorts:
Scorpio, Pisces
Possible prince:
Taurus, Virgo

76

## PRINCESS LEO

(24 July - 23 August) So Lilly.
Authoritative, creative, proud.
Leo, you were born to rule.
Everyone looks up to you,
and you never disappoint.
Best royal consorts:
Aries, Sagittarius
Possible prince:
Gemini, Libra

## PRINCESS VIRGO

(24 August - 23 September)
Altruistic, dedicated, persuasive.
If it's foreign policy or a formal ball,
you always get what you
want, Virgo.
Best royal consorts:
Taurus, Capricorn
Possible prince:
Cancer, Scorpio

## PRINCESS LIBRA

(24 September - 23 October)
Totally Tina.
Artistic, rational, diplomatic.
What's fair is fair, Libra,
and you always know it.
Very important for a princess!
Best royal consorts:
Gemini, Aquarius
Possible prince:
Leo, Sagittarius

## PRINCESS SCORPIO

(24 October - 22 November)
Powerful, practical, loyal.
Nobody enjoys the throne more than you do,
Scorpio, what with all the sceptre wielding.
Best royal consorts:
Cancer, Pisces
Possible prince:
Virgo, Capricorn

## PRINCESS SAGITTARIUS

(23 November - 21 December)
Progressive, giving, optimistic.
Who else do the people turn to in times of
woe, Sagittarius? You are depended upon.
Best royal consorts:
Aries, Leo
Possible prince:
Libra, Aquarius

## PRINCESS CAPRICORN

(22 December - 20 January)
Ambitious, confident, lively.
Will your kingdom triumph?
With you on the throne,
Capricorn, success is certain.
Best royal consorts:
Taurus, Virgo
Possible prince:
Scorpio, Pisces

### Friday, April 30, the Plaza

I entered Grandmere's suite super carefully, looking around for any cameramen or purple-haired girls who might be lurking in the shadows.

But Grandmere seemed to be the only one in there. Well, Grandmere and Rommel, who I discreetly checked for mics. But he appeared not to have any secret bugs tucked into his purple velour sweatsuit. That I could find, anyway.

'Oh, for God's sake, Amelia,' Grandmere said, apparently realizing what I was doing. 'They're gone. You made your position on the subject perfectly clear yesterday. There isn't going to be any television show. At least, not one featuring you.'

'What do you mean?' I asked, throwing down my backpack and making myself comfy on the couch.

Grandmere raised an eyebrow at me. 'Amelia,' she said. 'Feet.'

I took my feet off her coffee table. I guess the mean elf inside me is also kind of a slob.

'What do you mean, at least not one featuring me?' I asked.

'Well,' Grandmere said, 'you didn't want to go. Although you didn't have to have your mother telephone your father, you know, Amelia. You could simply have TOLD me you didn't want to appear on *My Super Royal Sweet Sixteen*.'

'I DID,' I said.

'In any case,' Grandmere said, 'it was too late to change all the plans I made for your party, so Lewis has arranged for another young person to take your place.'

'Another young person?' I gaped at her. 'Like who? A Mia Thermopolis lookalike?'

'Certainly not,' Grandmere said with a soft snort. 'Instead of your sweet sixteen, we'll be celebrating the sweet sixteen of someone else – a young man named Andy Milonakis.'

My jaw dropped. 'You're taking ANDY MILONAKIS to GENOVIA?'

'There's no need to shout, Amelia. And yes, I am. Lewis is very pleased with the way things have turned out. I'll be taking this boy and ten of his friends – I thought one hundred was a bit excessive, considering he's not even a family member – to Genovia, to do all the things you and your friends could have done for YOUR birthday, if you weren't so selfish and stubborn. They're calling it

*Andy's Super Royal Sweet Sixteen.* Lewis promises that it's going to reach millions of viewers. The glories of Genovia will soon be known to that hard-to-reach eighteen-to-thirty-nine-year-old-male demographic.'

For once, the little mean elf in me was silent. It didn't, for instance, goad me into suggesting that the eighteen-to-thirty-nine-year-old males who enjoy Andy Milonakis's show probably still live at home with their parents and can't afford a trip to Genovia.

It didn't prompt me to mention that the ten friends Andy would be bringing with him to Genovia were probably going to include – at least judging from his TV show – his dog, Woobie, the guy who owns the cherry-ice stand on the corner, and Rivka, the rooster-headed chicken lady, this old woman Andy forces to wear a hat with two chicken legs sticking out of it.

It also didn't urge me to tell Grandmere that Andy Milonakis probably turned sixteen ten years ago and was just using her to get publicity for his show, the same way she was using him to get publicity for Genovia.

Instead, I said, meaning it, 'Grandmere, this is the best birthday present you've ever given me.'

To which Grandmere replied with a slight snort and a sip of her Sidecar.

But I could tell she was pleased.

## Saturday, May 1, 10 a.m., the Loft

Well. That's it. I'm sixteen. At last. I can now legally have sex in most European countries, including Genovia, and just about every state in America. Except the one I actually live in.

Oh, yeah, and I can apply for a learner's permit to drive. Which I guess would be a big deal, if I didn't have to go everywhere in a limo anyway.

Mr G made real homemade waffles for breakfast, and then he and Mom and Rocky all sat around the table and watched me open my presents from them, which included, from Mom, a vintage Run Katie Run T-shirt; from Mr G, an iTunes gift certificate for fifty song downloads (yes!), and from Rocky, a big pile of Mead wide-ruled composition notebooks with black marbled covers, for future journal entries and novel-writing attempts.

Even Fat Louie got me something – a Fiesta Giles action figure to replace the one I sold on eBay to get Michael an original 1977 *Star Wars* poster last Christmas.

Oh well.

Mom apologized on Dad's behalf for his not having called or got me anything, but said he hadn't forgotten – he's just been super busy with Parliament.

I said Dad already got me a present – he yelled at Grandmere and got me out of having to be on *My Super* Royal *Sweet Sixteen*.

That is a gift for the ages.

Then Michael called and asked if I wanted to have the romantic birthday dinner I'd suggested we have in the first place. I said yes, and went to begin beautifying myself. Because even though our dinner isn't for eight hours, it never hurts to get a head start on the beautifying. Especially if you need a lot of beautifying, the way I do.

## Saturday, May 1, 5 p.m.

I've received birthday emails from around the world! Not just from my friends (although I've heard from all of them too – well, all except for Lilly, but that's no surprise; she's probably still sulking over her big chance to appear on MTV being blown), but from other royals such as Prince William and some of my Grimaldi cousins, including the one no one even knew I had, another illegitimate royal just like me, only this one courtesy of Prince Albert of Monaco.

But best of all was the CUTEST e-card from Princess Aiko of Japan, my favourite royal of all time (besides my dad, of course), of a chihuahua wearing a tiara.

Just had a lovely afternoon of made-for-TV-movie viewing . . . which is the best way to spend any birthday, if you ask me. Saw a Kellie Martin double feature, *Her Last Chance*, in which Kellie plays a teen drug addict falsely accused of her boyfriend's murder, and *Her Hidden Truth*, in which Kellie plays a teen delinquent falsely accused of her family's murder.

Good stuff.

Now I seriously have to get ready. Michael will be here to pick me up in one hour. I wonder where we're going to dinner????

SWEET SIXTEEN *continues on page 86*

# CLUED-UP PRINCESS

### Solve the clues and fill in the grid!

**ACROSS**

5. She teaches Mia how to act like a princess
6. and 1 Down. Cinderella's lost shoe (5,7)
7. Famous hotel where Mia has her princess lessons
8. Michael is Mia's ONE TRUE ____
9. Princess Mia writes in hers every day

**DOWN**

1. See 6 Across
2. King's wife!
3. Author of THE PRINCESS DIARIES series (3,5)
4. Mia's favourite world-saving charity

For solution see page 92

81

# The basics

- **Make sure** your parents have OK'd the event.
- Tell everyone to bring a **sleeping bag** and pillow. Comfort is utterly essential.
- Have lots of **yummy goodies** to eat (must include popcorn and ice cream).
- Have a pile of **DVDs** to watch (don't forget *The Princess Diaries* movies!). There's safety in numbers, so go for scary movies too!
- You should have some ideas for games. **Truth or Dare** is always a good one, so is **Who Am I?** (tape the name of someone famous on to your guests' backs and see if they can work out just by asking 'yes' or 'no' questions.

## More ideas to turn your sleepover into a total success:

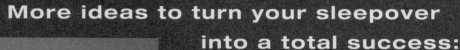

- **Beauty bar:** Get everyone to pool their make-up – then give each other makeovers! Try some daring new looks – flick through lots of mags for inspiration. If you can get hold of a Polaroid camera you can take before and after shots.

  A **hilarious variation** is to make each other up while blindfolded. Everybody will look really dumb – and the person who looks the worst gets a prize.

- **Nail night:** Give each other hand massages (so relaxing!), then manicures. Paint your nails crazy colours – maybe each guest could bring a different colour . . ., Or do your own **nail art**. It's not that hard! Just paint your nail in an under-colour, e.g. silver. Wait for it to dry (v. important), then cut up little sections of masking tape and stick over the bits of your nail that you want to remain silver. Finally paint a different colour over the exposed bit of nail, wait for it to dry *really hard* and then peel off the tape to reveal funky nails! A stripe looks cool, or perhaps a diagonal across the nail with a different colour either side

# PRINCESS MIA'S VE

**NO reading ahead . . . just answer the questions in order!**
When you choose names, make sure it's people you actually know.
Go with your first instinct. Get a pen and DO THIS NOW!

## INSTRUCTIONS

- Beside numbers 1 and 2, write down any two numbers.

- Beside the 3 and 7, write down the names of members of the opposite sex.

- Write anyone's name (like friends or family) in the 4th, 5th and 6th spots.

- Write down four song titles in 8, 9, 10 and 11.

1  4

2  6

3  Ben Poolman

4  Leonora O'hanlon

5  Granny mac.

6  Poppy Harper.

7  Jack stimpson.

8  Crazy in love

9  Fill my little world

10  last request

11  Walking on sunshine.

84

## ANSWER KEY

1. You must tell (the numbers in spaces 1 and 2) people about this game.

2. The person in space 3 is the one that you love.

3. The person in 7 is one you like but can't work out.

4. You care most about the person you put in 4.

5. The person you name in number 5 is the one who knows you best.

6. The person you name in 6 is your lucky star.

7. The song in 8 is the song that matches with the person in number 3.

8. The title in 9 is the song for the person in 7.

9. Space 10 is the song that tells you most about YOUR mind.

10. The 11th answer is the song telling you how you feel about life.

### Saturday, May 1, 11 p.m., Rockefeller Center

I've been had. I can't believe they ALL knew – well, everybody except Grandmere – and none of them said anything . . .

Oh well. I guess it's no more than I deserve, being such a party pooper and all.

Only, if I had known in advance about THIS party, I wouldn't have pooped on it. I SWEAR! It's like they all got together and tried to figure out what all my favourite things were, and then –

Well, OK, better start from the beginning:

Michael showed up at six on the dot for our date – even though I'd told him it wasn't necessary to pick me up, since I am perfectly capable of meeting him somewhere, given my limo and personal bodyguard. But he'd insisted. It never occurred to me to wonder why until we stepped outside (with Lars, who kept smirking – but I just assumed that was because he'd got Janine-from-MTV's phone number . . . I'd caught him text-messaging her the day before) and got into the limo and Michael didn't even tell the driver where to go.

But Hans started heading Uptown anyway, like they'd already agreed on their destination.

'Michael,' I said, starting to get suspicious. Actually, I'd already been a little suspicious something might be going on when Mom and Mr G, right before Michael arrived, had announced they were taking Rocky to see the latest *Winnie the Pooh* movie over at the Loews Cineplex. I mean, the kid is barely one. And they were taking him to the movies? At night?

But I wasn't thinking about that when the limo started heading Uptown without Michael saying anything.

'Where are we going?' I asked him.

But he just grinned and took my hand.

It was when the limo hit Midtown that I started getting even more suspicious. Michael can't afford to take me out to eat anywhere in Midtown. Anywhere I'd want to go anyway.

And then when the limo pulled up alongside Rockefeller Center, I REALLY started freaking out. Where could we possibly be going in or around Rockefeller Center? The rink was closed on account of it being too warm now for ice skating.

Except . . .

Except that as we pulled up to it, I saw that it wasn't. Closed, I mean.

Instead, the skating rink was closed *in* – with a giant white tent, like the kind people rent for weddings.

Seriously. The rink at Rockefeller Center was covered in a giant white tent. People were standing all around it, taking pictures and pointing, like the tent had just magically mushroomed there overnight.

You couldn't tell what was going on underneath the tent. But you could see there were lights on in there. I thought maybe there was a fashion show or a special episode of *The Apprentice* being filmed there, or something.

Except that the limo pulled over right next to the stairs that head down to the rink. And Michael got out of the car, then held the door open for me to follow.

'Michael,' I said, 'what is going on?'

'Come and see,' he said, still grinning.

And he took my hand and led me out of the limo and down the steps to the rink, and the entrance to the big white tent . . .

. . . where a member of the Royal Genovian Secret Service bowed and lifted the flap for us to enter –

– into a winter wonderland! Seriously! Even though it was the first of May, the ice across the rink was hard and smooth! The air inside the tent was chilly – it was being cooled down by about a hundred portable air conditioners! There were snowmakers in every corner, sending flurries of white snowflakes into the air . . . snowflakes that were glistening in the hair of this huge group of people standing out on the ice, who all shouted, at the same time, 'Happy Sweet Sixteen, Mia!'

I couldn't believe it! A surprise birthday ice-skating party! There was my mom, and Mr G, and Rocky, and Lilly, and J.P., and Tina, and Boris, and Shameeka, and the guy Shameeka has been dating this year, and Ling Su, and Perin, and the Drs Moscovitz, and my neighbour Ronnie, and even, of all people, my DAD!!!

I never suspected that they were planning something . . . something other than Grandmere's horrible *My Super Royal Sweet Sixteen* thing.

And I certainly never would have expected an ice-skating party on my birthday, seeing as how it's just slightly warm out for skating!

But trust Michael to find a way to give me EXACTLY what I wanted.

Well, pretty much, anyway.

After I'd screamed at everyone for keeping such a big secret from me, I found out that none of them had actually known about it, except for Michael, who'd come up with the idea and arranged the whole thing, and my mom and Mr G, who'd been in charge of making sure I was in the dark about it. And my dad, who'd paid for it . . . as well as for twenty stationary bikes, which he was donating in my name to AEHS, so we could have spin classes instead of volleyball from time to time . . .

It's not enough to create a personal workout and health programme targeted to every student's own specific health needs. But it was a definite start!

Principal Gupta is going to die when they're delivered on Monday.

Everyone had a good laugh over my indignation at Grandmere's plan. 'Like I was ever going to let her do any such thing,' was what my dad had to say about it (he said he'd tried to invite Grandmere to the skating party, but that she'd declined the invitation. I didn't tell him that was because she's busy taking Andy Milonakis to Genovia. I figured he'll find that out on his own, soon enough).

Even Lilly was like, 'You didn't REALLY think I was in on her scheme to put you on MTV, did you?'

Um, yeah. I really did. But I didn't tell her that. Finding out that she really hadn't been was a totally awesome birthday present – but one that made me feel totally terrible when, while we were all chowing down on cake and lacing up our skates, Lilly came over to me and whispered, looking super weird, 'I did it. I told him.'

At first I didn't think I'd heard her right, because they had the sound system turned up so loud, with Rihanna's 'Pon De Replay' blaring. Then I noticed her expression, which was a mixture of dismay and total embarrassment. And I realized what she'd said.

My God. She'd drunk the fat. LILLY DRANK THE FAT!!!!

Even Ross didn't drink the fat, when Rachel asked him to. He was GOING to, but at the last minute, she stopped him . . .

Only I hadn't got a chance to stop Lilly from drinking the fat. Because I had never in a million years thought she'd go ahead and do it. I mean, we're best friends and all.

But that she'd actually gone ahead and DRUNK THE FAT??? I couldn't believe it.

'You TOLD him?' I practically shrieked.

'Shhhh!' Lilly pinched me. A birthday pinch to grow an inch, I guess. 'Not so loud! Yes, I told him. That's what you wanted, wasn't it? That's what you said I had to do so you could trust me again. So I did it.'

And then I felt the little mean elf that had sprung alive inside me the day before die a quick, ignominious death. What had I been thinking? Why had I asked Lilly to do something so stupid – and humiliating? Telling J.P. she loved him wasn't going to keep her from cheating on him with some other random guy, as she'd done to Boris, or keep her from mortifying me at this, or any other future event. I can't believe I'd asked her to do something so stupid . . . so practically guaranteed to make him run from her like a startled fawn.

But even more, I couldn't believe she'd actually done it.

Glancing over to where J.P. – who was turning out not to be the world's best skater – was being coaxed by Lars to let go of the rink wall, I asked, 'What did he say? When you told him, I mean?'

'Thank you,' Lilly said softly.

'You're welcome,' I said. 'I knew if you were just honest with him about your feelings, it would all work out.' I'd actually known no such thing, but it seemed like the right thing to say. 'But what did he say?'

'That's just it,' Lilly said, still not looking very happy. 'He said thank you.'

I blinked at her. 'Wait . . . you told J.P. you love him, and all he said back was thank you?'

Lilly nodded. She still looked . . . funny. Like she didn't know whether to laugh or cry.

And honestly, I didn't know which she should do either.

'Not exactly an explosion of passion, huh?' Lilly said.

'Not exactly,' I said. What could J.P. be thinking? Who says thank you to someone who says they love you? Especially to someone whose tongue has been in your mouth?

Then, because the whole thing was my fault really, I said, 'But it could be, you know, that he didn't know how to reply. I mean, on account of him not being used to having a girlfriend. Or any sort of human interaction aside from his parents.'

Lilly brightened a little. 'You think?'

'Totally,' I said. And, since Michael had skated up to us at that very moment, I went, 'Hey, Michael, if a girl tells a guy that she loves him, and the guy says thank you, that means he's just not used to that level of intimacy, doesn't it?'

'Sure,' Michael says. 'Or that he's not that into her. You got a second?'

'J.P. is TOTALLY into you,' I assured Lilly, who looked like she was about to kill Michael. 'Seriously. Stay here, I'll be right back –'

Then, skating away with Michael, I said, 'Why'd you have to say that? She just told J.P. she loves him, and all he said was thank you!'

'Huh,' Michael said, pulling me to the far side of the rink. 'Bummer for her. Open your present now.'

'My present?' All thoughts of Lilly and her romantic travails left me. 'Michael, I thought this party was my present! It's so fantastic . . . the snow, the skating, you and me . . . how did you know this is exactly what I wanted?'

'Because I know you,' Michael said, leading me off the ice until we stood in front of a huge box I hadn't noticed before. And I do mean huge. It was taller than me practically. 'Open it.'

I opened the enormous cardboard box and found, standing inside it – 'A Segway Human Transporter!' I shrieked.

'Uh,' Michael said quickly, 'not really. I mean, it's a human transporter, but not a Segway. We promised to make each other gifts from now on, remember? So I made you a self-balancing scooter – it's just like a Segway, with the same safety features, redundancy and fool-proofing, but it's not the actual—'

'Oh, Michael!' I cried, throwing my arms around his neck. I seriously felt like crying, I was so happy.

Especially when '(I've Had) The Time of My Life,' from the *Dirty Dancing* soundtrack, came on over the sound system and I looked out across the rink and saw my mom skating with Mr G . . . and Tina skating with Boris . . . and Lars skating with Janine (don't ask me where she'd come from) . . . and Shameeka skating with What's-His-Name

. . . and Perin skating with Ling Su (I'll think about that one later) . . . and Dr Moscovitz skating with Dr Moscovitz, even though they were arguing over the collective unconscious . . . and even my dad skating with Ronnie (I'm sure Ronnie will tell him she used to be a man sometime) . . .

But, best of all, J.P. skating with Lilly, and not running from her like a startled fawn, in spite of her having told him that she loved him.

'Come on, Michael,' I said, pulling him back out on to the ice. 'Let's have the time of our lives.'

And so we did.

## THE END

# SOLUTIONS

## CROSSWORD Page 24

### ACROSS
1. Ariel  5. Britney  6. Pocahontas
10. Hathaway  13. Lilly  14. Pea

### DOWN
2. Etiquette  3. AEH  4. Cat  5. Bodyguard
6. Planet  7. Charming  8. Sixsational
9. Ball  11. Palace  12. May

## WORDSEARCH Page 25

## CROSSWORD Page 81

### ACROSS
5. Grandmere  6. Glass  7. Plaza
8. Love  9. Diary

### DOWN
1. Slipper  2. Queen  3. Meg Cabot
4. Greenpeace

## MAZE Page 44

## WORDSEARCH Page 45

# DON'T MISS THESE OTHER FANTASTIC MEG CABOT BOOKS!

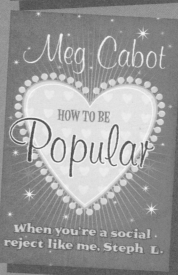

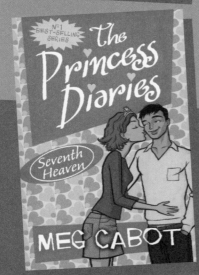